THE MINIATURE GOLF COURSE MURDERS

Sara Penhallow

Copyright © 2014 Erin M. Hartshorn

Cover Font: Strange Newes created by Feòrag NicBhrìde, licensed under a Creative Commons License.

Cover images credit: Erin M. Hartshorn

Published by Eimarra Press

Bethlehem PA

All rights reserved.

For T and R—and for Kaky, again

CHAPTER ONE

Wednesday, June 16, late morning

Isobel Santini stood off to one side of the cash register at the Five-and-Diner, tapping her toes while she waited for the soup order she'd called in forty-five minutes earlier. Peak lunch rush shouldn't have been for another half an hour; what was taking them so long? At least the delay kept her out of the office a little bit longer — Gerri Hess, the executive editor and publisher of the college press and thus Isobel's boss, had been on a tear lately. If you defined lately as "since she got back from her last vacation."

A few extra minutes was good; more than that, not so much. As managing editor of River Corners College Press, Isobel had plenty to do under normal circumstances, and these were not normal. Not only was Gerri being demanding, but also Isobel's assistant was out sick *and* Isobel had a date this evening, which meant that she wanted to leave early today. Hence the take-out order — she had planned to work through lunch at her desk. She still would, but she wasn't saving any time by doing it.

A nasal voice from one of the nearby tables caught Isobel's attention. She didn't have to peer through the plastic plants to identify the speaker — Sadie McKenzie, well known for her opinions on everything having to do with Saint Theresa's parish, second only to Sue Holstein, the mayor's wife, in her interfering ways.

"—and then he told me I was wrong about the doctrine!"

The measured tones of Father Paul answered her. "He was correct, Sadie. As long as he's not trying to re-marry in the Church, there's nothing I can do about it."

Sadie's voice rose. "Of course not. You've already done enough, haven't you? If you hadn't gotten involved, we'd still be married in the eyes of the law, not just the eyes of God!"

Isobel glanced around, looking for somewhere to move so she could avoid listening to this conversation. The divorce of Kyle and Sadie McKenzie—and subsequent marriage of Kyle McKenzie to his secretary, Rita Black—had been both acrimonious and very public. Isobel had already heard quite enough details. Unfortunately, the diner wasn't large enough to escape anyone bent on creating a scene, so she stayed where she was.

Father Paul's voice stayed calm and level. "I did nothing I should not have done."

"You told him to divorce me!"

"Do you really believe I would betray my faith and my vows like that?"

"He went to you for counseling, then came back and told me he wanted a divorce. What else am I supposed to believe?" Her voice dropped again, but it was still loud enough to carry. "You're a damned hypocrite, and you ought to be defrocked."

"I'm sorry you feel that way." A chair scraped. "I met with you because I hoped to ease some of your pain, but if you're not willing to let go of it, there's nothing I can do. I need to get back to work now."

No takeaway bag had miraculously appeared to allow Isobel to effect an escape. The priest, clad as ever in black with a Roman collar, passed the plants Isobel stood near and stopped at the register to pay his bill, Isobel nodded politely at him and did her best to look as though she hadn't heard the entire conversation. With his hair going silver at the temples, he looked very much a benevolent priest. He probably wasn't fooled by Isobel's pretense—he never had been—but he gave her a half-smile and return nod.

Now, would her lunch be ready before she had to face Sadie?

Another chair scraped, and Isobel's heart sank. No way out of this. Instead of seeing Sadie, however, she heard another voice, pitched low—"Sue's been worried about you, Sadie. Is there anything we can do?"

"Sure—make sure Father Paul has nothing to do with the festival!"

The mention of Sue and the invocation of the upcoming festival—Summerfest, jointly sponsored by the town of River Corners and River Corners College—identified Sadie's new companion as none other than His Honor Richard Holstein, mayor of River Corners. Isobel had known Richard all her life (part and parcel of growing up in a small town), and her only complaint about him was his execrable taste in women. Isobel didn't have much use for his wife Sue.

"You know I can't do that. The chaplain at the college always does the opening prayer."

"Can't you—I don't know—say something about separation of church and state, and say that we're not going to have prayers this year? That man is insufferable."

A burst of laughter from further back in the diner covered up the next few words, and then the bell between the kitchen and the front rang. "Order up!"

Isobel looked over hopefully, but two plates with burgers and fries sat waiting to be taken to a table. She slumped against the cash register, resigned to listening to more of Sadie's whinging.

"—can't change tradition," Richard was saying.

"Why not?" Sadie replied. "We do it all the time. We didn't have Santa at the Christmas pageant, did we?"

Silence descended on the diner, and Isobel winced. "Santa" had been a murder victim the previous year, so the lack hadn't been a willful departure from tradition. Sadie was just lucky the widow—Isobel's best friend—wasn't here.

The next voice wasn't one Isobel knew. "If you're finished with your meal, could you perhaps continue your discussion elsewhere?"

"You have open tables. You don't need this one." Sadie's voice was vicious. "Or are you trying for an even lower tip?"

The speaker must be Sadie's waitress, then. She tried again. "You're making our other customers uncomfortable."

"Did any of them care when my husband made me *uncomfortable* by dumping me for another woman? Do any of them care about the hypocrisy openly practiced—"

Richard cut her off, but his voice was low enough that most of the diner's customers probably couldn't make out his words. Isobel, thanks to her location, could. "Sadie, if you keep this up, the only friends you're going to have in town are Sue and me. Maybe you should consider trying a fresh start somewhere else?"

"I've already lost my husband, and you want me to lose my home and my job as well?" Sadie's voice rose again. "You're just afraid being associated with me is going to hurt your chances for re-election, and you want to get rid of me."

She had a point. Richard had already begun his re-election campaign, and for a change he wasn't running unopposed. He didn't need anything that would drag his name into the mud.

Of course, that meant that he wasn't very likely to accede to Sadie's requests. If he tried to interfere with the college's contributions to the festival, he'd be starting another round of town-gown disputes. Then there would be the local people who firmly wanted things to stay the same (such as Isobel's Momma and Aunt Rosa—who would both be scandalized by the lack of an opening prayer). Richard couldn't take the chance that they'd be miffed enough to vote against him.

Sadie didn't seem to get that, though. "If you really want to get rid of me, want me to go away, do what I'm asking—get him away from the festival. After Summerfest's over, I'll move away and you won't have to worry about me torpedoing your chances."

"I can't, Sadie. You know that."

"Then don't be surprised if I do something myself." Her chair scraped backward. "Say hello to Sue for me. I don't think I'll be seeing her again."

Hurriedly, Isobel stepped away from the cash register to give Sadie room to pay her bill. Although Sadie was older than Isobel, she didn't look it. Since her divorce, she'd gotten her hair cut and colored, gone in for Botox injections, and hired a personal trainer—as if any of that would get Kyle back. Still, Isobel admitted that Sadie looked amazing with the chic asymmetric cut to her blue-black hair and her tailored pants—casual enough to work in the florist shop, but sharp enough for evening wear.

Sadie gave Isobel a sidelong glance, but quickly focused on the red-headed waitress who had started cleaning the counter. "A little service here, please?"

The waitress stiffened, but she continued what she was doing. Isobel's lips twitched; the waitress clearly hadn't appreciated the comment about an even lower tip. Had Sadie left one at all?

The manager—a frazzled looking man with curly red hair, quite obviously the waitress's father—looked out from the pass-through to the kitchen. "Kari, you have a customer."

The waitress straightened up, but she took her time putting away the cleaning rag she'd been using. The manager didn't reprimand her.

"How was your visit today. Was everything to your satisfaction." The words were wooden, delivered—Isobel was certain—because the waitress was required to ask, not because she cared.

Sadie snorted; she understood exactly what the waitress meant. Instead of answering, she pushed money across the counter and stood there, tapping her fingers impatiently while the waitress counted it to be sure it was all there. Finally, the waitress pushed some buttons, counted the money into the drawer, closed the drawer, and tore off the receipt. She handed it to Sadie with a mechanical smile. "Thank you. Have a nice day."

Isobel noticed that the waitress didn't say, "Come again."

The door jangled as Sadie passed out. The waitress glanced at Isobel. "You can grab a table or a seat at the counter."

Isobel shook her head. "I'm waiting on a take-out order. I called it in about an hour ago."

"An hour! You would've eaten faster if you had sat down. Let me check on that for you."

Isobel smiled gratefully. She hadn't been here the whole hour, but she did want to get back to work soon if possible.

Three minutes later, the waitress handed her a to-go bag. "The cook put it in a container and then got distracted. No charge," she added as Isobel pulled out her wallet. "Not after that long a wait."

"At least let me give you a tip."

The waitress smiled broadly. "Customers like you are a pleasure to have."

Instead of people like Sadie. Isobel didn't blame the waitress one bit, but she did need to get back to her desk and start dealing with her own recalcitrant people, from vendors to her boss.

CHAPTER TWO

Wednesday, June 16

When she got back to her office on the lower level of the college's old infirmary, Isobel opened her lower desk drawer and tossed her messenger bag inside. If her assistant Violet were here, Isobel would have regaled her with the unpleasantness at the diner, but that wasn't an option today. Instead, Isobel made a mental note to send her assistant flowers later. Looking at the large stack of material sitting in the inbox, she added chocolate to the gift—she wasn't looking forward to sorting the mail herself this week.

It could wait another twenty minutes while she ate her lunch and sorted through everything that had landed in her e-mail while she'd been out. If she played her cards right, it could even wait until tomorrow morning; she certainly had enough other things to do.

Her e-mail wasn't any more compelling—the top half dozen messages were campus-wide broadcasts started because *somebody* had parked in the dean's parking spot, and even if he weren't here, his secretary saw it as her duty to defend the spot against all comers. Just as riveting were the reminders about the dorm renovations, notices about plant facilities, and requests for sublets from students who had forgotten they'd need somewhere to stay over the summer.

She was tempted to delete the entire inbox without reading, but there were probably a couple of messages that actually needed her attention—such as the one from Gerri asking for spreadsheet data to present at the budget committee meeting later in the week, and three increasingly frantic e-mails from one of Isobel's favorite freelance copyeditors about probable plagiarism in the manuscript she was working on. She opened the offending manuscript.

The Miniature Golf Course Murders

Isobel had sent a rejection to this author, telling him the manuscript, as it stood, was not publishable and needed more work—reorganization, better references, and a more reader-friendly tone (which was more tactful than saying "No one wants to have a pompous ass condescend to them"). The author—the assistant to the vice-president of finance, who occasionally filled in as an adjunct in the business department—promptly complained to Isobel's boss. Gerri would make nice with anyone who controlled the purse strings; she accepted the manuscript with a terse "Make it work" directed at Isobel.

Easy enough for her to say.

First things first—Isobel sent an e-mail back to the copyeditor, thanking her for bringing the matter to Isobel's attention, asking her to stop working on the manuscript for the time being, and reassuring her that she would be paid for her work regardless of what happened. Next came the hard part—verifying the problem.

The copyeditor had documented specific paragraphs—and in one case, an entire subsection of a chapter—where the voice had changed and a quick Internet search brought the text up under somebody else's name. If those were the only problems, this could be salvaged—but first, Isobel had to find the scope of the plagiarism. She logged in to CrossCheck, a commercial service for detecting plagiarism, similar to the Turnitin service some of the professors used for term papers, and launched the iThenticate tool.

The tool page reminded her that the service only worked for selections of less than fifty pages, which meant that she would need to break the file up. Fortunately, she had a macro set up to divide files by chapter (useful for some portions of her workflow), but running the checks chapter by chapter was going to kill the rest of her afternoon. She consoled herself with the thought that at least now she didn't have to feel guilty about ignoring the physical mail piling up in the inbox.

She uploaded the first chapter, selected the checkboxes for it to be checked against the broader Internet as well as the CrossCheck and iThenticate databases, and stood up to make herself some tea. A cup of Earl Grey would be perfect, with its citrusy scent of bergamot to keep her calm. Maybe she'd grab some cookies from the vending machine at the end of the hall to go with the tea.

Her stomach rumbled at the thought. Why was she so hungry? She'd gone out...she turned around slowly. The take-out bag from the Five-and-Diner sat right where she'd placed it on the corner of her desk. After waiting so long for it, she'd still managed to forget to eat. Sighing, she crossed to the desk and picked up the bag. The soup would reheat fine in the microwave.

This did mean she should give the cookies a miss, though, at least for now.

Isobel settled back down at her desk, the cup of Earl Grey tea on her left and the reheated bowl of soup on her right. Just as she put the first spoonful of soup in her mouth, the phone rang. She swallowed hastily.

"River Corners College Press, Isobel Santini speaking. May I help you?"

"So formal!" Her momma's voice came over the line. "Did your Caller ID stop working again?"

"Hello, Momma. No, I just didn't want to spill my soup—"

"Soup? You're eating real food for lunch, and not something you scavenged from some machine?"

"I usually eat real food!"

Her momma snorted but said nothing.

Isobel sighed. "It's from the diner. You *know* I eat there at least two or three times a week."

"When you learn to cook enough so you have leftovers—"

"Let's get me to the point where I can cook well enough to want to eat leftovers, first."

"And how are we going to do that when you never come to visit?"

Suppressing another sigh, Isobel pushed her soup away. No question, she was going to have to reheat it again. "I was over this weekend."

"Certainly you were, after church with Michael and my sister—not exactly ideal circumstances for your next lesson. Unless you want your cousin to mock you every step of the way?"

As if that would have stopped Momma! Isobel knew she was probably more worried about her sister learning her recipes. Aunt Rosa would say that she didn't care, she was a better cook than her sister anyway—and that was an argument both Isobel and her cousin Michael knew better than to get involved in.

"Of course not."

"So? When are you coming? You do remember that you're supposed to cook Thanksgiving dinner in five months, don't you?"

Five months. Isobel swallowed. She'd been working on her cooking all year, but she still didn't think she was going to be ready for that level of responsibility.

"Help you cook it, you mean," she said.

"I don't believe that's what I said." Her momma's voice was frosty. "Unless you think you know better than me what I said?"

Isobel rubbed her forehead. She *so* did not need this. Meekly, she said, "No, Momma, of course not. But five months doesn't seem like very much time—"

"It certainly isn't if you don't come over for your cooking lessons! Tonight, then?"

"I can't." Without giving her momma a chance to cut in, she said, "Greg's taking me out tonight."

Greg was Greg Stone, who had joined the history department as an assistant professor the previous fall. Greg and Isobel had met just after the first of a pair of murders tore that department apart.

This time, her momma's sniff was softer. She approved of Greg, even if she hadn't said so recently, at least as much as she approved of any men. "Out to dinner?"

"Maybe. He said he was going to take me out to do something fun."

"Out?"

Her arch tone implied that they normally stayed in to do something fun. Isobel blushed but sidestepped the implication. "Somewhere away from the office. He said I need to loosen up a bit."

"I'll just bet he did."

"Momma!"

Her momma chuckled. "Not tonight then, but how about this weekend? Not Sunday, for obvious reasons."

Meaning to avoid Isobel's Aunt Rosa and cousin Michael. "Aren't we having dinner at Aunt Rosa's on Friday?"

"Saturday, then—unless spending time with Greg is more important than visiting your aging mother and letting her pass on the family traditions..."

Isobel rolled her eyes. "You're not that old, Momma. Can we make it Saturday evening? Greg wants me to go house-hunting with him in the morning."

"Oh."

"Oh"? What was that supposed to mean? Ohhh!

"Not like that—not together! Greg's been subletting from Ron Davis, who's been out of town on sabbatical—you remember, he was spending the year in Kiev? Greg needs to move out before Ron gets back."

"Oh, that's all right, then." Glad she thought so. "Saturday evening. Come as early as you can because you're making dinner."

Satisfied at having the last word, Momma hung up. Isobel made a face at the phone before placing the receiver back in the cradle. She wondered whether it was worth digging through her messenger bag for her cellphone to see if her momma had left a message on voice mail this time before calling Isobel's work number. She supposed she should—if Momma had had anything to say, she would expect Isobel to know the message by heart.

After Isobel dumped the contents of the bag in front of her computer (which was waiting for her to enter the file for the next search), she reconsidered her decision. Why in the world did she have that many pens? But there was her phone—no messages, of course, but the phone showed she had missed Momma's call. She must have left the ringer silenced after Mass on Sunday.

She turned the sound back on, set the phone next to her tea, and dumped the rest of the pile back in her messenger bag. She could sort out the dozen different shades of red pen later.

Once that was dealt with, she dropped the messenger bag back into the bottom drawer and returned her attention to her computer. iThenticate had given the first chapter a clean bill of health. That made sense; it had been the most confusing morass Isobel had ever seen. No one would have published it in that shape. She uploaded the next chapter, then took a bite of soup.

Yes, cold again. Maybe she'd manage to get lunch eaten before Greg picked her up, but it wasn't looking too likely at the moment.

CHAPTER THREE

Wednesday, June 16, mid-afternoon

A couple of hours later, Isobel finished running the plagiarism checks and began compiling the information into a document. At least a quarter of the book was cribbed from other sources without attribution (even in the bibliography), and a further ten percent was from papers the author himself had written but the journals of publication owned the copyright to. Isobel rubbed her forehead and reached for her teacup.

The cup was empty; time to make more tea. That would give her a chance to stretch her legs and think about how best to present this to her boss, too. Gerri had been clear that it was Isobel's job to make this work, but she was reasonably certain that didn't mean she was supposed to rewrite the book from scratch—although the idea of hiring a ghostwriter looked more and more feasible.

More than a third of the book!

She stood up and stretched, then grabbed her cup and crossed over to the tea area. As she unwrapped a tea bag to place in her cup, her boss's voice came from the doorway. "You haven't sent me the spreadsheets I asked for."

Isobel took a deep breath and let it out slowly before turning around and answering. "I'll get them to you before I leave today."

Her boss looked perfectly composed as usual, her ash blonde hair hanging in neat waves and her navy blue suit as crisply pleated as if she'd just that moment taken it out of the closet. Immaculately plucked eyebrows drew down in a frown. "I thought I made it clear those were a priority. What could you possibly have to do that was more important?"

Any of the other dozen responsibilities Gerri had saddled Isobel with in the past two weeks? Isobel swallowed that response. "One of the manuscripts has extensive plagiarism issues, and I've been determining the scope of the damage before settling on a plan of action."

"Plagiarism? You should be more careful what manuscripts you accept. Really, Isobel—"

This time, though, Gerri had gone too far. "I *didn't* accept it. In fact, I told the author that it wasn't publishable in its current form—and that was before the plagiarism was discovered. You, however, told me I was wrong, and now I'm trying to deal with the mess you handed to me."

Isobel bit the inside of her lip. Everything she'd said was true, but she didn't usually talk back to her boss. She returned her attention to the teabag rather than meeting Gerri's eyes.

"I see." Gerri's voice was flat. "Then deal with it—and *do* get me those spreadsheets today."

Of course Gerri wouldn't have any suggestions on what to do—and heaven forfend that she should take responsibility for her own mistake. But when Isobel glanced around to ask for ideas, Gerri was gone.

And no doubt expecting the spreadsheets within the next thirty seconds, rather than sometime before the end of the day. She wouldn't get them quite that fast, but Isobel moved them to the top of her to-do list—right after making this cup of tea and getting those cookies from the vending machine after all.

Isobel actually went through two more cups of tea (and decided against a second package of cookies) before the spreadsheets were ready to send to Gerri. Usually, Violet updated the sales figures twice a month, and the vendor information weekly. With her out sick, it hadn't gotten done, and Isobel had to track down all the numbers, which in turn meant logging in to Violet's computer and accessing her e-mail (thank goodness for saved passwords!). By the time Isobel hit "Send" on the message to Gerri, she was ready to call it a week.

Instead, she picked up the phone and dialed the local florist.

"River Corners Flowers. We put a smile in your day!"

Isobel blinked. "Kimberley? What are you doing there? Aren't you busy enough already?"

Kimberley Ansel, Isobel's best friend and landlady, was a successful event organizer, much in demand for parties, weddings, retirements, and pretty much anything else that needed coordination of different people around town. Currently, she was working on Summerfest, which seemed like plenty on its own, even without two weddings every weekend of the month. She didn't work for the florist.

"Isobel! What are you up to?" Kimberley's voice turned sly. "Ordering flowers for a certain professor?"

"No, for Violet. But why are you working at the florist?"

"Oh, I just agreed to step in for the afternoon. Sadie had something she wanted to do, and she asked if I could *please* fill in just a couple of hours. Since I know the stock at least as well as she does, I agreed."

Sadie again. Whatever trouble she was stirring up this time, it wasn't Isobel's concern.

"Can I get a bouquet sent to Violet—whatever the usual 'Get well' bunch looks like? And on the card, have it say, 'Get well soon to rescue me from the dragon!'"

Kimberley laughed. "That good, huh? Okay. Of course, your flowers are going to look pretty paltry next to the ones your cousin picked out."

"Kimberley Jean, are you trying to upsell me?"

"Would I do such a thing to my best friend?"

"Only if you thought you could get away with it," Isobel said dryly. "I don't care what Michael picked out for her."

"Right." Kimberley's tone said that she didn't believe a word Isobel had said. "Okay, I'll send you a bill. Sadie prefers that I not take people's credit card information over the phone."

"Oh—can you add a pound of chocolates to that?"

"Sure thing. I'll tack it onto the bill. It's still not as nice as what Michael sent."

Laughing, Isobel hung up and opened the plagiarized manuscript again. She'd been mistaken—verifying the plagiarism hadn't been the hard part—tedious, perhaps, but not hard. The hard part was going to be dealing with the author. She opened her e-mail and started a new message (without a recipient, so it didn't get loosed on the world unintentionally).

"While working on your manuscript"—no, that would get the copyeditor involved in this discussion, and that wasn't the freelancer's job. Isobel erased the start.

"Irregularities have surfaced"—barf!

"Your manuscript is lacking many references in the bibliography section, which we will be adding. Additionally, we will require permissions from the copyright-holders of the following articles by you to include selections from the articles in the manuscript." Not a bad start, but she still needed to come up with a way to mention all the sections he'd copied from other people's work. Maybe this would be a good time to go through the mail. It needed to be done, right?

Unfortunately, her earlier triage had already dealt with all the important messages. She shoved vendor solicitations into a folder to check out later when she needed new suppliers or freelancers, trashed all the spam, and found herself facing a severely depleted inbox.

Maybe she should go down to the vending machine for that second package of cookies after all? She tapped a pen against her desk consideringly.

No, she shouldn't procrastinate any longer. She went back to her e-mail program.

Taking a deep breath, she typed, "Sections of the book that are verbatim quotes of other authors' work will need to be rewritten in your own words before we can continue with the copyediting. Please let me know how much time you will require for this work so I can adjust our work calendar accordingly."

It wasn't the best e-mail, but it did avoid outright accusing the author of plagiarism, which was the important point. Well, the second important point, the first being to get the plagiarism dealt with so the book could actually be published. Isobel pushed "Send."

CHAPTER FOUR

Wednesday, June 16, later in the afternoon

"Knock, knock." Greg stood in the doorway, tall with sandy brown hair and gold-rimmed glasses. His hands were tucked into his khaki pockets. "You ready to go?"

"Mentally? *So* ready. Physically? I need to logout and grab my bag." Matching her words, she moved the mouse to click on the logout command.

A second voice interrupted—Gerri again. "You're leaving early? What about those spreadsheets?"

Isobel paused without clicking. "I sent them hours ago."

"I didn't get them." Gerri's voice dripped with disbelief.

Gritting her teeth, Isobel re-opened her e-mail program. "See for yourself." She pointed at the message in her sent mail.

Gerri said, "I still didn't get them. Send them again."

She'd probably set up her system to quarantine any messages that came in with attachments, not trusting the campus's antiviral scanners to do their job. Or maybe just because she was clueless about technology.

"I'll just give you a copy now." Isobel didn't want her evening with Greg disrupted by a series of phone calls from Gerri, all about how the spreadsheets still hadn't arrived. She opened the large door of her desk and rummaged through the kipple for a flash drive.

"I don't want—"

Isobel tuned out the rest of her boss's protest. Gerri wanted the spreadsheets, she could have them and good riddance. It took Isobel less than a minute to plug in the drive, copy the files to it, and remove the drive. She handed it to Gerri.

"And now, I am leaving. I told you Monday I would be taking an early day today, and I've already made up the time."

More than made it up, but this wasn't the time to fight that battle. She'd wait for her next employee evaluation session, although with any luck, Gerri would have moved on to worries other than Isobel leaving early one day of the summer.

Gerri sniffed. "Everything had better be here." She pushed past Greg on her way out without even a nod of acknowledgment.

Greg's eyebrows flashed upward. "One of those days?"

"One of those months. Give me just a moment, and I'll be done here."

After she'd locked up her office, they strolled out of the building together. "We can take my car," Greg said, lacing his fingers through hers. "I parked over in the lot on Main."

"Where are we going?"

"I thought we'd go minigolfing."

"Putt-putt golf? Really?"

"Why not? It's relaxing, it's fun, and it doesn't matter how well you play."

"Ha! You never played with Michael."

"Somehow, it does not surprise me that your cousin is cutthroat."

She laughed out loud and leaned her head against Greg's arm. "Only when our mothers are not around." They had almost reached the edge of campus, and ahead of them stood a woman with a clipboard. Isobel groaned. So this was what Sadie had to do when she asked Kimberley to watch her shop.

"Not a big fan of petitions?"

"Petitions themselves don't bother me. It's just—Sadie. I've already had my fill of her today."

He tugged at her hand. "Come on, we can walk right past."

"I doubt it," she muttered.

She was right. Sadie saw them coming and stepped into the middle of the sidewalk, feet spread apart to take up more space. "Sign my petition to have the opening prayer removed from Summerfest."

"No." Isobel moved to push past her, but Sadie was undeterred, turning to focus on Greg.

"There's no reason to have religious overtones at a community celebration of summer. It makes people of different faiths uncomfortable, and it has nothing to do with the festival."

Greg wavered.

"Nonsense!" Isobel snapped. "You know as well as I do, Sadie McKenzie, that we've had opening prayers by Rabbi Rebecca Lippman, the Lutheran minister, that visiting Buddhist nun a few years back...whoever the college currently has acting as chaplain. You're just trying to stir up trouble."

"We don't need a prayer," Sadie insisted. "Summer has nothing to do with religion."

All of this because Sadie was angry at Father Paul? Isobel dug deep, looking for compassion for the level of pain the other woman must be in, but instead she found herself channeling her inner Momma. "Some of us don't decide God is irrelevant when he's inconvenient." Sniffing, she pulled at Greg's hand. "Come on."

He didn't say anything until they'd gotten into his car. He ran the air conditioner with the windows down for a minute to clear out the hot air that had accumulated during the day. Finally, putting the car into gear, he said, "I didn't realize you felt that strongly."

She shrugged, uncomfortable. "I don't know. Raised Catholic, go to Mass every week, plus on Holy Days of Obligation and my saint's day. She's not quite as regular an attendee at Saint Theresa's, but she's there once or twice a month. She's just mad right now."

"Maybe you could give her the benefit of the doubt. If she's a reasonably good Catholic, maybe she's doing this because she believes it."

There wasn't much traffic on Main Street, but Greg didn't immediately pull out. Isobel could feel him looking at her, but she didn't meet his eyes.

"No. It's just to get at Father Paul. She blames him for her divorce, thinks she and Kyle would still be happily married—well, married, anyway—if it weren't for him. I'd be willing to bet she's writing letters to the bishop to try to get him reprimanded, too. She was yelling at him at the diner this afternoon!"

He sighed and turned left out of the parking lot. "I think you're being too hard on her."

Isobel grimaced and fidgeted with the buckles on her messenger bag. He didn't know Sadie, or Father Paul, the way she did. How could he? Time to change the subject.

"Momma wants me to come over Saturday afternoon for my next cooking lesson. I told her you'd already spoken for my morning."

"Hmmm. If it means edible food, maybe I should let her have you for the full day."

The corners of his lips twitched as he tried to keep a straight face. Isobel gave a long-suffering sigh. "You've obviously been spending too much time with my cousin. You've never even tasted my cooking!"

"I understand I'll live longer that way." This time the smile broke through.

"Are you going to be in town for the big Thanksgiving Day reveal, or are you going to be visiting your parents?"

"Michael has advised me to be out of town if at all possible, but my mother said they wanted to come see where I'm working. You won't mind a couple more people at the table, will you?"

No pressure or anything—just her first major family meal ever, and she was supposed to cook for her boyfriend's parents, too. "No." Her voice came out as a squeak. She swallowed and tried again. "The more, the merrier."

"You don't have to," he said. "My mother would be more than happy to cook a dinner and meet your mom some other point on the weekend."

This talk of their mothers meeting made her feel light-headed. They weren't *that* serious yet, were they? But it had been half a year now, which was a record for her. Too gun-shy because of her dad, Michael said.

She looked over at Greg again, wondering how to tell him how confused she felt. He flashed her a grin, and she returned a small smile. They could talk about this later. Thanksgiving was still months away.

They lapsed into a comfortable silence as they headed east from the town center. Only a few houses sat on this stretch of road, interspersed with a small grocery store, the Baptist church, and a walk-in clinic the college helped pay for so people didn't have to drive forever to get to an emergency room. (Oddly, college students seemed to need one fairly steadily. Or maybe not so oddly, given some of the things she and her friends had gotten up to.) Just beyond the town limits—where the regulations were a little looser—sat a used car dealership ("Butler's Used Cars! See US First!" as if there were that many choices in town) and the miniature golf course.

"Have you considered that?"

Greg's question came out of nowhere, and Isobel shook her head in confusion. "Considered minigolf? I thought that's why we're here."

"No, I meant a new car. Well, a new used car. If you get a convertible like that little blue one, you'd be more likely to notice when you leave a Christmas tree sitting on the roof."

She looked in the direction he pointed. The convertible was cute, but not really her style. And the price painted on the windshield—"On my salary? Get serious. Besides, around here, you don't use soft tops in the winter."

"It's something to think about, anyway," he said. "And you could get a hard top."

"I *like* my car." She knew she sounded defensive, but Greg had the sense not to push the issue.

"We're here."

The lot was far from full, but Isobel was still surprised by the number of cars in it. A glance at the course showed several teens in clusters, divided between the front and back courses.

Loud voices came from inside. Isobel's shoulders tightened. She'd had enough of angry scenes today; this was supposed to be relaxation. Maybe they could go somewhere else instead?

Greg put his hand on the small of her back and steered her toward the door. Fine. The argument wouldn't follow them out onto the course itself.

White paneling lined the room inside. A wooden counter divided the employees' section with its bins of putters from the public section, which was large enough to hold a couple dozen people.

"—just a sign." Richard Holstein, an election sign clutched in one hand, stood at the counter, talking to the guy behind the counter whose shirt proclaimed him to be Brian.

"I understand that, Mr. Holstein," Brian said, "but I'm just the manager. You need to talk to the owner, Gina Metzger."

Richard didn't give up. "It's not even Miss Metzger's property. It's the verge."

"You know the rules for signs. If it's out there, we're responsible for it. You need to talk to Ms. Metzger. She's the one who'll have to deal with any comments from Mr. Butler about not being neighborly."

"When will she be in? Can I just leave the sign with you, so she can put it up?"

Brian ignored the questions to look at Greg and Isobel. "Howdy, folks. You want nine holes or eighteen?"

"Let's live dangerously," Greg replied. "Give us the full twenty-seven."

Richard turned and nodded at the pair of them, and Isobel nodded back. He seemed completely at ease—but then, that was part of what made him a good politician. No matter where he was or what he was doing, he was genial and affable—not charismatic enough to make the leap to the state assembly, as much as that would thrill his wife—but more than enough to keep him in office here in River Corners. Still, he must be worried about the outcome of the election, or he wouldn't be out here now.

"Been here before, then?"

"No, I just checked you out on-line." Greg pulled out his wallet. "Nice website, by the way. I like the animations of the different holes."

"Thanks. That was my idea." Brian handed them each a putter with "Metzger's Minigolf" engraved in gold script on the handle, as well as a scorecard and pencil. "Remember, if you get the ball in on the last hole, your next game is free."

They stepped through the side door into the actual course, and Isobel let out a breath she didn't know she had been holding.

"You okay?"

She nodded. "Sorry. Ran into Richard—and Sadie—earlier today, when she was making the life of everyone at the diner unpleasant. I had to wait forever for my lunch."

"Ah. That's why you were so hard on her."

She shrugged, then reached into the bucket of balls next to the door and pulled out a bright yellow one. "Anyway, I was surprised to see him here. Usually, he's got a huge crop of volunteers that Sue runs ragged."

"Sounds like a woman who needs something to do with her time."

Isobel laughed shortly. "She spends most of it scheming to take over Kimberley's business. She can't even do most of the work—being the mayor's wife means she couldn't get the contracts because of the nepotism laws—but that doesn't stop her from trying."

"She can't just disclose a conflict of interest?" He waved for her to go before him on the first hole, a simple sloped zigzag, so she carefully set her ball down on the white dot.

"Nope. No conflict of interest, no recusals. No nepotism allowed. It goes back to this rumrunner during Prohibition."

She lined up her shot and putted before stepping to one side so he could take his turn. Her ball banked onto the second leg of the hole, but didn't go very far.

"A criminal made River Corners pass laws against nepotism?"

Isobel waited until after he'd taken his shot before answering him. His ball stopped only a few inches from the hole. "The sheriff was the oldest son of the mayor. When the sheriff had to step down, no one else wanted to take his place…"

"And the rumrunner got to keep delivering alcohol."

"All very legal and aboveboard," she assured him. "Aside from that pesky little Amendment."

He laughed. "I love this town. So why hasn't the law ever been taken off the books?"

"It may have a weird reason for existing, but it makes some things simpler." She nodded at his ball. "Your shot."

He readied his putter but paused to meet her gaze. "Like keeping unpleasant people away from jobs you don't want them to have?"

"In case you haven't noticed, there's not a shortage of unpleasant people in town. Or on campus even," she added, thinking about Gerri.

His ball dropped into the cup. "Oh, yes, I've noticed. Believe me, I've noticed."

CHAPTER FIVE

Wednesday, June 16 (still)

They played three more holes (a windmill, a sphinx, and the leaning tower of Pisa) before Isobel asked Greg about his comment. "Been running into more unpleasant people in the history department?"

He chuckled. "What, the blackmailing former chair wasn't enough? No, actually, the department itself is fine. We all have different areas of expertise, so we don't even get into academic arguments most of the time, and it's not like we have a lot of money to fight over."

Isobel stared at the low bridge of the next hole. The artificial turf split in two directions on the other side. If she tapped the ball too hard, it would take the longer route to the hole, but if she didn't hit it hard enough, it would just roll back down on this side of the bridge. There always seemed to be some perfect spot to hit the ball, and she never found it. Sighing, she hit the ball just a little harder than she thought she needed to.

It reached the arc of the bridge, teetered, and stopped.

"I'm supposed to get my ball past yours?" Greg asked. "Can we just put a marker down?"

"What do you think this is, pro golf?"

He gave her a mock glower before striking his ball at an angle to bank off the side of the bridge. It rolled down, looking as if it were headed directly for the short route, but his angle hadn't been quite right—the ball struck the concrete curb where the paths diverged and continued rolling down the long path.

Isobel bounced gleefully up the bridge. She might actually come out ahead on this hole! "Who's being unpleasant to you, then?"

The Miniature Golf Course Murders

"Oh, you know, it's just interdepartment fighting. Sociology wants another adjunct, and they don't think it's fair that we've got three at the moment."

"That's only until you've replaced John and Peterson, isn't it?" She paused before swinging and raised her head to look at him, but he was looking off at the car lot next door.

"Yes, but that's another year—we put the notice out too late to hire this spring. Most applications won't even be in until this fall, and then we'll have to go through the hiring process, including all of the interviews and get our choice vetted by the dean, then hope the one we want didn't get a better offer somewhere else..." He trailed off with a shrug, then met her eyes. "It's a little unusual to be doing a search for two positions right after they hired me, and 'Your predecessor was murdered by a jealous colleague' isn't exactly a selling point for most applicants. It could take longer than a year to get someone new."

She thought about that while she took her shot. Her ball struck the concrete curb in almost the same point his had, but hers rolled down the short path. She grinned. She might even beat par on this hole!

"Have you told sociology that all they need to do to get more adjuncts is have their department turn into a hotbed of crime?"

"No, but I've considered hitting *their* department chair over the head to make her shut up about it." He snorted. "It would certainly make some of the faculty meetings more interesting."

Isobel chuckled. "Sounds like most of the meetings on campus." She tapped her ball again and was rewarded with a thunk as it dropped into the cup. "Three!"

"Did you know what you were getting into when you took a job back here? About what it would be like working at the college, I mean?" He looked at her curiously, leaning on his putter rather than lining up his shot.

"I don't know." She turned her own putter in her hands, uncomfortable at his scrutiny. "All jobs have bosses and pressures and budgets, and deadlines are a way of life for presses. So I think I figured it wouldn't be that much different at the college press from working for any other publisher."

"And is it?"

"I don't know," she repeated. "Maybe. I mean, we have to justify our budget to the college and the board of trustees instead of shareholders, and I'm sure if I were working at a publisher somewhere else, I wouldn't be getting e-mails about dorm rooms and whether the dining commons should have the same food sourcing that the faculty cafeteria does. But there would be other things to drive me crazy."

He re-focused his attention on the ball, gently tapping it back toward the divide. It stopped right in the middle, and he hit it toward the hole. Clunk. "Three for me, too."

Greg picked up his ball, then straightened and put his arm around her. "I'm glad you came here."

She leaned into him. "Me, too." Then, "As if Momma would've let me go anywhere else. You know she and Aunt Rosa ganged up on me."

"I'll have to send them flowers." He kissed the top of her head, and they strolled toward the next hole.

Laughter from near the end of the course caught Isobel's attention, and she glanced over. A teenage boy grabbed the brunette who had laughed and kissed her.

"Wasn't she at the Christmas party?" Greg asked.

Isobel looked again. "Yes, that's Annie. I don't remember if that's the boy she was with, though."

Putting his arm around her shoulder, Greg said, "She's got time to settle down."

She tilted her head to look up at him and was only mildly disappointed when he merely squeezed her and let her go, rather than kissing her. "True enough."

He nodded toward another couple on a different hole. "Popular date activity."

"There's not a whole lot else to do in town, once you've seen the movie releases," Isobel said. "Not as a teen."

"Did you come here often, then? With Dante?"

She grinned. "Sort of. The back course was just then under construction. John, Kimberley, Dante, and I would meet up at somebody's house and sneak in after dark. It was easier to scale the fence then—the car lot wasn't next door, so they hadn't surrounded the course with the thirty-foot chain-link yet."

"Tsk. Did you get caught?"

"We-ell, there was the time Michael found us sneaking back home. He wasn't exactly happy."

Isobel busied herself with placing her ball on the white spot. This next hole was deceptively easy—a straight shot, with no obstacles except that the hole was on top of a sloping mound. Her first stroke knocked the ball halfway up the slope. It hesitated, then rolled back down and came to a stop two-thirds of the way to the hole. Her shoulders slumped; it was going to be one of *those* days.

Her second stroke took the ball right over the top and down the other side. When the ball finally dropped into the cup, she was at eight strokes for the hole.

"The scorecard says the max is six," Greg pointed out.

She gave him a mock glower and left the eight where she had marked it.

"What did Michael say when he caught you?" Greg lined up his own shot, which went right down the middle and stopped on the edge of the cup.

"Oh, he was all Michael—we were lucky we weren't arrested for breaking and entering or vandalism. And the lecture went on for at least half an hour."

He chuckled. "Did he turn you in?"

"Are you kidding? Both of our mothers would've blamed him for not stopping me." She gave a snort of laughter. "Which didn't stop him from threatening to tell them if he caught us again."

His ball dropped into the cup, and he leaned over to pick it up. "How long before you sneaked out again?"

She raised a hand to her chest and widened her eyes in mock innocence. "Would I do that? After my own cousin impressed on me the need to behave myself?"

"Next day, huh?"

"I'm sure we waited at least two or three days so he wouldn't be suspicious."

"He's probably *still* suspicious."

"You might have a point there."

They kept playing. Isobel lost her ball into the pond on the eighth hole and had to go back to the building to get another. This time, she went with sky blue.

"You'll never find that if it goes into the water."

"I'm just going to take a six on that hole and go on to the last one."

"Live a little."

She shook her head. "We've got another eighteen holes to go after this, remember?"

"All right. Watch how it's done." Greg hit the ball smoothly down the artificial grass. It looked like he might get a hole in one this time, but the ball sailed clean over the cup, hit the concrete curb on the far side, bounced up, and headed straight for the pyramid at the ninth hole.

Isobel kept a straight face as she strolled over to pick it up. "Two stroke penalty." She straightened up and noticed a panel on the side of the pyramid protruding. "That's odd."

"Can I have my ball back?"

"In a minute," she said over her shoulder. "I just want to peek inside. Haven't you always been curious?"

"I can see why you don't have a cat. You'd be too similar in temperament. 'It's a door. I must see what's on the other side.'" But he walked up behind her. "So what's inside?"

The panel, which actually was a door, but one with a latch rather than a knob, seemed stuck. If her cousin were here, he probably would've just pushed it all the way closed. Isobel tugged twice, hard, knowing that it would be hard to convince the manager this had been only idle curiosity. Finally, the door came open, making her stumble backward into Greg, who steadied her.

She thrust her head inside, blinking to try to adjust to the darkness. Light filtered in past her shoulder, as well as a little from the holes carved into opposite sides of the pyramid for the ball to traverse.

"I think there's someone in here," she said quietly. Then, louder, "Are you all right?"

She stepped inside and bent down to touch the person's shoulder. The head lolled toward her, and she saw the familiar features of Father Paul, marred by the blood that had run down from the top of his head.

CHAPTER SIX

Wednesday, June 16

Isobel leaned against the chain-link fence, staring at the pyramid. Until Michael got here with his officers, she had to make sure no one else went in.

Greg stood next to her. "It's not your fault, you know. He was probably dead before we got here."

"I saw him at lunch today. It's just…"

"Hey, who's that leaving?"

"What?" Isobel swung her head around to see two cars pull out of the parking lot. "Michael's going to be pissed." She frowned. "Stay here? I'm going to go see what's going on."

She stormed into the building. "What are you doing?"

Brian shrugged. "Working."

"You were supposed to keep everyone here."

"Look, all I have is your word for it that I was talking to the police. This wouldn't be the first time we've been pranked, you know—and no one's shown up yet, have they?"

His tone was so dismissive Isobel had to take two slow breaths before answering him. She still hadn't decided what to say when the door from the back course opened and Annie came in with her friend. Breathing a sigh of relief, Isobel turned to her. "Annie, you remember my cousin, from your grandparents' farm before Christmas? He's coming here, and he doesn't want anyone to leave before he gets here."

"Ha! Your cousin. I knew it!" Brian crowed. "You are punking us."

Annie's eyes widened, and Isobel knew she was thinking about the reason Michael had been at the Christmas tree farm—a murdered body. She'd know soon enough that was the reason here, too.

Annie sniffed dismissively at Brian. "You've obviously never met her cousin." She turned to Isobel. "We'll just sit over there on the bench, if that's okay? And I'll make sure everyone else knows not to leave."

"Thanks." Isobel gave her a small smile. "I'm heading back outside. Let him know when he—"

The front door opened, and Michael strode in, not quite hitting his head on the lintel. He frowned at her. "Isobel, I thought I told you to keep an eye on the scene."

"I was. But then Brian here—" She nodded in the employee's direction. "—decided this was just a prank and let people leave."

If Michael had been mildly annoyed to see her inside, now his expression was thunderous. He strode over to the counter, placed his fists on it, and leaned over Brian. "Does this uniform look like a prank? You will give me the names of the people you allowed to go, you will call someone else—preferably your boss—in to take your place here, and then you will go downtown with a couple of my officers."

"You can't make me."

Michael glanced over his shoulder at the officers who had followed him inside. "Cuff him. I'll decide when I get back whether to charge him with obstruction."

"You can't do this," Brian said, jerking his arms away from the officer who had gone behind the counter. "I know my rights. You have to charge me with something, and I get a phone call."

"No, I don't," Michael glanced at him dismissively. "You can be held twenty-four hours without being charged. If you're not charged, you don't get a lawyer." He turned to Isobel. "Show me."

She led him outside. "It's in the pyramid. I left Greg watching it when the cars drove away."

He led the way across the course, going around plants and hazards, but making as straight a line as possible. "It's been a while since I've been here, but isn't the pyramid closed?"

"Usually." She could feel him looking at her, but she didn't look up. "But this door in the side was open a crack, and I just wanted to see…"

"I want to tell you that you ought to keep that curiosity in check, but if you had, there's no telling when the body would have been discovered."

"In this heat? It probably wouldn't be too long." She wanted it to be a joke, had tried to make it one, but her voice shook too much. The reality of another dead body was settling in.

He reached out and squeezed her shoulder. She relaxed a little.

"You said it was Father Paul? Why would anyone kill him?"

She snorted. "Obviously, you weren't at the Five-and-Diner today. Sadie McKenzie was giving everyone an earful on why he's the worst thing that ever happened, how he should be ashamed of himself, and so forth."

"The divorce?"

Isobel nodded. "The divorce."

"I'll have one of my officers stop by her place to question her. She got the house in the divorce, right?"

They'd reached the pyramid, and Greg stepped forward to join them. "You have a suspect already?"

"Everyone's a suspect," Michael said. "Except maybe Isobel. She'd drive around town with the murder weapon in the passenger seat for everyone to see."

Isobel gave a long-suffering sigh. "One Christmas tree, and you'll never let me forget it."

Michael and Greg exchanged grins. "Can't you keep her out of trouble?" Michael asked.

Isobel answered. "About as well as you ever did—and by the way, it's not my fault someone killed Father Paul."

"You didn't have to find the body!"

Isobel shook her head. "Not now." She pointed at the side of the pyramid. "Through there."

Michael pulled a glove from his pocket and pulled it on before nudging the door open. "We'll have to have Madge in to check it out."

"You don't think he's dead?" Isobel's voice rose in a squeak.

"We need the scene examined—what was he killed with, was he killed inside the pyramid or put there afterward, how long has he been dead? The usual."

There shouldn't be a usual. River Corners had gone years without a murder, and now, they had their second murderer in less than a year.

"Okay, I'll have a couple of officers sweep the courses, make sure everyone's accounted for and sent to the building. Keep an eye on this until they get here, would you? I need to go see if I can find the phone number for the owner, who's almost certainly going to be as annoyed with me for hauling that character off as for the dead body on the property."

"The dead body's not your fault."

"I'll still get blamed."

"Gee, I wonder what that's like?" Isobel said, and Michael gave her a wry grin before striding off.

When he opened the door to the building, his voice carried across the course. "What's he still doing here?"

The door closed behind him, but Isobel wanted to know what was going on. It sounded like Brian had talked the officers into letting him stay. She gave Greg an apologetic look and opened her mouth to ask him to stay put.

Before she could say anything, however, he said, "Go on. I'll hold the fort. Or the pyramid, anyway."

She smiled her thanks at him and sped after her cousin.

When she got to the door, she opened it just enough to slip inside and sidle along the wall. Michael saw her and shot her a frown, but given that he was in the middle of yelling at most of the rest of the room, she counted that as mild annoyance.

"You don't trust the police to close up the shop properly?"

"No, not really," Brian said. "You can't put the register in the safe, you wouldn't total the day's receipts, and you would probably miss one of the doors when locking up. And if anything goes wrong, I'm the one Ms. Metzger will blame, not you."

"Fine. Give me Ms. Metzger's number, I'll have her come down to deal with everything, and you can take the blame for *that*," Michael growled.

"I can give it to you, but it won't do any good. She's on vacation—her niece is getting married in Maui, so she took two weeks off."

Two weeks in Hawaii sounded good to Isobel.

"And she left you in charge while she's gone?" Michael looked skeptical.

"I'm a good worker," Brian said defensively. "I notice things, I have ideas—I even put our website together."

Michael's snort left no question what he thought about a website. "Fine. You can stay here until we're done, do your receipts, lock up, and *then* we'll take you down to the station."

The Miniature Golf Course Murders

"Very generous."

If Michael noticed the bitterness in Brian's voice, he gave no sign of it. Instead, he turned to one of the officers who was taking the names of Annie's group. "Speed it up, will you? And when you're done here, head next door to the car lot. See if Butler or his salespeople saw anything. Get their names and contact information while you're at it."

"You should probably check out the house across the street, too," Brian volunteered. "I think it's been empty for a while, but it can't hurt."

"The old Heming house in the trees?" the officer asked. "It's been empty for ten years at least!"

Brian shook his head emphatically. "No, there was someone there this spring. They'd come in at lunchtime, sometimes again in the evening. Didn't stay overnight, as far as I know."

Michael pinched the bridge of his nose. "We'll check that out, too. Thanks."

Just then, Madge—the county coroner—came through the front door, trailed by officers carrying tool boxes. Most likely her gear. "Isobel! I hear you found another body for me."

"I knew it!" Annie exclaimed.

Michael's groan was audible. He'd probably wanted to keep the news quiet for as long as he could. He spun and faced the teens. "You will not tell anyone what happened."

"You mean no one except our parents, right?" Annie's boyfriend asked. "You wouldn't keep something like this from your mom, would you?"

A couple of the officers tried to hide their smiles. The possibility of Michael keeping anything from his mother was virtually non-existent—and the penalty for trying would be guilt-trips for the foreseeable future. Aunt Rosa and Momma were alike that way.

"I suppose," Michael said grudgingly. He pointed at Annie. "As long as your mother understands this isn't an invitation to come down and ask questions."

Annie's mother was a photojournalist, who after being embedded with a unit in the Middle East took a tour of Southeast Asia on her own and had now returned home to work on a book based on her experiences.

"I'll tell my grandmother. She'll understand."

Michael nodded. "All right. After you've given your information to the officer, you may go. But I don't want to hear about this from anyone else."

31

They voiced assent in standard teen dialect—"Yeah, sure," "Whatever," and similar expressions.

Madge grabbed Isobel's arm. "Why don't you show me where it is, while he finishes up here?"

"Miss Santini," Annie called, "how did we miss it? We went through the course not that long before you did. There wasn't a body."

Isobel glanced at Michael for help. She was sure he didn't want to give out any details, and she didn't want the teens' parents to be blaming her for their nightmares about bodies on the course.

He shrugged. "Where would you hide a body?"

"In the pond!"

"Don't be silly—it's not deep enough. Besides, your ball would have bounced right off the body and into the next hole."

"The windmill?"

"Not big enough. Maybe the sphinx."

"The door on the side of the pyramid is broken—"

Michael looked sharply at Annie's boyfriend. "And how do you know that?"

The boyfriend's eyes got large, and he scooted back on the bench, so he was against the wall. "Everyone knows it. It's been broken for months. Some of the kids from school use it."

"For?" Michael raised one eyebrow, and Isobel was glad she wasn't on the receiving end of that look this time.

"What do you think?" the other boy answered him. "Drinking, smoking, fooling around—it's all good."

The girl he was with scooted away from him. "All good? How much have you been doing?"

He opened his mouth and shut it again.

"I see." Her voice was icy. Isobel was willing to bet this was their last date.

Madge said, "Thanks. That's good to know when the forensics team goes over the scene. We won't expect clean DNA evidence, that's certain." She tugged on Isobel's arm. "Come on. You were going to show me, remember?"

"As soon as you have, I want you to go home, Isobel. I'll send an officer over to get your statement later."

"Can I go to Momma's instead? You know she's going to hear about this, and—"

"Don't remind me." He rubbed his forehead. "Fine, go there. I'll drop by when I'm done here."

CHAPTER SEVEN

Wednesday, June 16, fading into evening

In the car, Greg squeezed Isobel's knee. "I'm sorry about this. The date was supposed to help you relax."

She gave him a wry smile. "Not your fault. And I haven't been worrying about work, so that's a plus."

He shot her a concerned look. "Are you in shock? We can stop somewhere and grab you some hot tea, lots of honey or sugar. Or maybe coffee?"

The thought of sugar in her tea made her stick her tongue out. "Just take me to Momma's. She'll have something on hand, and you know she'd be insulted if I stopped anywhere else first."

He chuckled and started the car. "It's good to know there are some things you can count on."

The drove in silence for a few minutes, heading back up Main Street and then south toward the street where Isobel had grown up.

Isobel snorted. "At least Sadie got what she wanted—Father Paul's not going to be doing the opening prayer."

"You don't think she murdered him, do you? That seems like an awfully trivial reason to kill somebody."

"Probably not." Isobel leaned her face against the window. The glass wasn't cool, though, and she sat back up. "I did tell Michael about the scene today, though; I figured he'd hear about it soon enough, anyway."

She paused for a minute, then said, "I wonder who they'll get to do the opening prayer now. The college won't have time to appoint a new chaplain."

"They probably have rules for this. They have rules for everything, including how to make new rules."

"Those are the important ones," Isobel said mock seriously. "Can you imagine how many rules they would have if there wasn't some sort of limit to how they could be created?"

"I shudder to think."

"The choice will probably fall to either Kimberley as organizer or to the mayor—who won't want to offend anyone, so will throw the choice at Kimberley anyway."

"And what would you advise, with your deep knowledge of how the town works? Who could do it and not have anyone else get upset?"

She knew he was teasing her, but she answered anyway. "Simplest would be to just ask another priest from Saint Theresa's to step in. They'd probably even be able to use his prepared prayer, assuming he's got a copy in his office at the parish. That's what I would do, anyway." Isobel reached out and fiddled with the air vents to blow more cool air onto her face. "I'm glad it's not my headache. I've more than enough on my plate as it is."

"So you have no intention of solving this murder?"

"Michael's welcome to it."

Aunt Rosa opened the door as Isobel approached. "I thought you two had a hot date tonight."

"Rosa, let them in!" Momma's voice floated from the kitchen. "Just because she would rather play a game than listen to me talk about gravies is no reason to be rude."

"I burned the flour last time," Isobel said sotto voce to Greg.

Her aunt heard anyway and gave Isobel a sympathetic hug as she opened the door farther, admitting them to the pastel peach and white living room. "Maria Elena's in the kitchen."

"Hello, Momma." Isobel walked through the room that served as her momma's public face and into the homey kitchen with its warm wooden hues and red accents. Baking supplies were clustered on one of the granite countertops near a full pot of coffee, and her momma stood at the butcher block island, a bowl of dough on her left and a stack of cookie sheets on her right. Isobel dropped a kiss on her momma's flour-dusted cheek. "Brutti ma bouni?"

The "ugly but good" cookies were one of her favorites, a wonderful blend of chocolate and hazelnut. Nutella on toast was the best she could do on her own, but that paled in comparison to her momma's baking. She sniffed the air. None were baking yet.

"Yes, I am making cookies. No, you may not have any. Yes, if you ask nicely, I will let you help."

Isobel smiled fondly. "Rolling out dough sounds wonderful right now. May I please help?"

"Do I look like I'm using a rolling pin? No, you have to pinch off the dough—just so much, you see?—and roll it between your hands. You'd think you had never watched me bake these before!"

"Sorry, Momma."

Isobel washed her hands at the sink, then came over to stand next to her momma at the island and begin working. Greg sat down on a stool on the opposite side of the island and watched with fascination as she rolled the small balls of dough and set them onto a cookie sheet.

After a few minutes of working in companionable silence, Momma said,"You never did answer your aunt. Why aren't you two off at the golf course?"

Isobel bit her lip, met Greg's eyes, then gave a big sigh. She'd been hoping to put this off longer. "I found another body."

"You what?"

"Did you tell Michael?"

Isobel answered her aunt first. "Of course I told Michael. I called him from the golf course. He's there right now, but he sent me home."

"Good. A murder scene's no place for you," Momma said. She glowered at Greg. "What were you thinking, taking her someplace like that?"

Isobel tensed. "He didn't know."

Momma shook her finger at Isobel. "I asked him, not you. Don't you go defending him!"

Isobel took the dough that was in hands and smashed it flat on the counter. "Then don't you go making accusations like that. Come on, Greg, we're leaving."

He didn't move. "So what are you making the cookies for? I don't think I've ever heard you refuse to give food to someone."

"Don't change the subject!"

Aunt Rosa said, "She won't tell me, so I doubt she'll tell you. I think she's baking them for the church, for after Mass on Sunday. You remember how she complained about the doughnuts last week?"

"Shows what you know," Momma told her sister. "They're not for the church. Besides, Mary Beth Scott is in charge of the refreshment committee, and she probably knows better now than to let her daughter do it for her. Can you imagine—supermarket doughnuts?"

Isobel's shoulders relaxed a little. Greg's gambit had worked, at least temporarily; her mother and aunt were distracted from talk about the murder. She hadn't thought this through—she didn't want to be the one to tell them the pastor was dead. She'd been so caught up in thoughts about Sadie and Summerfest that the bigger picture hadn't occurred to her.

"What are you planning to do with so many cookies, then?" Greg asked. "Sell them at the festival?"

Momma's cheeks grew pink, and for a moment, Isobel and Aunt Rosa just stared at her.

"If you're hard up for money, you can move in with me," Aunt Rosa said. "Or just ask."

Momma drew herself up even straighter than usual and stuck out her chin. "I am not in financial difficulty. If you must know, I'm doing it because I want to do it. I've always wanted to open a shop of my own, but—"

"But Papi always said his little princesses didn't need to work," Aunt Rosa said softly, "and you didn't want to disappoint him." The gentle tone from her aunt toward her sister startled Isobel, who was used to their abrasive manner with each other.

Momma nodded once, tersely.

Isobel threw her arms around her momma. "I'm proud of you, Momma. It takes courage to follow your dreams."

Momma stiffened. "Are you saying I haven't had courage before? Do you know how hard it is to raise a child on your own—especially a willful one like you?"

"No, and I hope I never have to find out," Isobel said honestly. "I've never doubted you were strong, Momma. Not ever."

Momma thawed a bit and returned the hug, patting Isobel on the back. "You certainly did your best to test my limits. Still do," she said, releasing Isobel with a frown. "Another dead body? Who is it this time? No one we know, I hope."

Tears pricked at Isobel's eyes. This was the part she'd been dreading. She opened her mouth twice, then sobbed. She couldn't get the words out.

"Look at you, brow-beating the poor child when she's obviously still in shock! Let her recover for goodness' sake." Aunt Rosa came around the island and rubbed Isobel's shoulders. "You should sit down, not stand here shaping cookies for my sister!"

Isobel shook her head and swallowed. Hoarsely, she said, "It helps to have something to do."

Momma dusted her hands off on her apron, then went to a cupboard and pulled down a mug. She poured coffee from the pot into it, then opened one of the lower cabinets and topped off the mug with a slug of brandy. She thrust the mug at Isobel. "Here, drink this, you'll feel better." She looked at Greg, "Do you need something, too? You don't look nearly as broken up."

"I'll have mine without brandy, please. I'm driving." He gave her a half-hearted smile. "I didn't know him as well as Isobel, so I'm not as broken up as she is. It is my first dead body, though, and it's a bit unnerving."

She poured him a cup of coffee and handed it to him along with a sugar bowl and cream from the refrigerator. "You did recognize him, then?"

Greg nodded somberly. "It was Father Paul."

Isobel had seen both Momma and Aunt Rosa face hard news before—when her father ran off, when Rosa's husband had died, when their own parents had died. She had forgotten how Momma would blanch, as all the blood drained from her face and she swayed on her feet, and how Aunt Rosa's eyes, always large and dark, became larger still. The keening sound they both made she had tried to forget, but found herself unable to.

She set her cup down untouched and placed one arm around both her momma and her aunt. The keening gave way to sobs, and the three of them cried together.

Finally, Momma pulled back and brushed at her eyes. "Who would do such a thing? He was a man of God!"

Aunt Rosa grinned. "I remember when he was just a man."

"Rosa! For shame!"

"What? I'm human. You can't tell me you never noticed how handsome he was."

Isobel stepped in. She didn't want to think about her mother and men. "Perhaps you should both have some coffee, as well."

The Miniature Golf Course Murders

Momma nodded and retrieved two more mugs from the cupboard. She put brandy in both, then splashed in a little bit of coffee on top. Aunt Rosa took a cup from her and gulped at it. After a moment, she lowered the cup and said, "You're right. We need to know who would do such a thing."

"Ha! Mark it on your calendar," Momma told Isobel. "She said I'm right."

Isobel permitted herself a faint smile. The pair would be all right.

"Only about this." Aunt Rosa frowned. She looked at Isobel. "I don't suppose you found the murderer conveniently standing over the dead body? Or a written confession pinned to his chest?"

Isobel shook her head. "Nothing so helpful, I'm afraid. The body was hidden away inside the pyramid—"

"And you found it? What were you doing in there?" Momma shook her head. "No, I don't want to know. I've heard what some of the teens get up to in that thing."

Was Isobel the only one in town who didn't know? Who would have guessed her momma knew more about popular make-out spots than she did? But she supposed that conversation at bridge games might well turn to "what is the younger generation coming to?"

"I just wanted to know why the door was ajar." She sighed. "At least we know it happened this afternoon, so that should make Michael's job a little easier, anyway, assuming the guy from the minigolf course remembers who all was there this afternoon—or cooperates and tells Michael."

"I don't think he was being deliberately obstructive," Greg said. "He didn't know he had a dead body."

Isobel's lips pinched together, and she leaned across the island at him. "I told him that the police were coming. I let him talk to Michael, who clearly identified himself."

"Yes, but he had no idea who you were. Why should he believe you?"

She stared at him flatly for a full half minute, giving him the chance to backpedal, but he didn't take it. "Do I look like the sort of person who would pull a prank on a business?"

Greg looked a little nervous, but he stuck to his point. "The best prankers don't. That's why they do it so well."

She turned away. He was just being reasonable, she knew, and normally she treasured that part of him, but right now, she needed to be emotional and the outrage kept the tears at bay. "Maybe you should go now. I'll have Michael take me home after he gets here."

As if her words had summoned her cousin, the front door opened and Michael called, "Hello! Have you all decided who did it yet?"

CHAPTER EIGHT

Thursday, June 17, morning

Isobel glared at her e-mail the next morning. The problem author had replied, but his reply was the opposite of helpful. "I don't understand your e-mail. Call me to discuss it."

She re-read the original message—simple enough to do, as he hadn't bothered to trim when he replied. No, she had been perfectly clear, even if she hadn't come right out and said that most of the book was plagiarized and couldn't be printed without both the press and the author being named in lawsuits. The contract with the author said that he was ultimately responsible for all lawsuits and judgements, but that wouldn't stop plaintiffs from naming the press as a co-defendant. Grrr. He was being deliberately obtuse.

His extension was listed in his e-mail signature, so she dialed him.

"Yes?"

How rude, she thought. "This is Isobel Santini, over at the college press," she began.

"Oh, yes," he said. "The woman who sent the confusing e-mail. I don't understand why you're bothering me with this. Your boss said you'd work out any problems in developmental editing."

Her hand tightened on the phone. She didn't know which one of the pair she was more upset with at the moment. "Large amounts of the text have to be rewritten from scratch because they're other people's words. That's ghostwriting, not developmental editing."

"So?" His tone made it clear that he considered it her problem, not his.

She gritted her teeth. How could he be so oblivious? "We don't have a budget to hire a ghostwriter. You'll need to pay for that yourself. I can recommend some ghostwriters."

"Can't you do it?"

"I'm not a ghostwriter."

"So hire one."

"We don't have a budget item for that," she repeated. "If I do that, I'll have to bill you for the cost."

"Hmph. I'll talk to your boss about this. I'm sure she can see sense." He hung up without saying good-bye.

Isobel hung up as well, shaking her head. Absolutely nothing had been accomplished. However, she hit "Reply" on his original e-mail and added Gerri as a cc. She began typing.

"To make sure we are on the same page, this summarizes our telephone conversation of this morning at 9:15.

"Much of the text needs to be rewritten to use new words and draw your own conclusions. This is beyond the scope of developmental editing and will require the services of a ghostwriter. As the press does not have the money to pay for such an expense, we will find a ghostwriter to do the necessary work, and the bill for services rendered will go to you.

"If I have neglected to include pertinent facts from our conversation, feel free to reply. Otherwise, I will commence the location of someone to provide suitable services for your book."

She left out his threat to call Gerri. He probably already had. It didn't matter; this was within her responsibilities. She sent the e-mail.

The next question was where to find a suitable ghostwriter. The best ghosts didn't advertise. She put out a couple calls for recommendations on editorial mailing lists, then sent an e-mail to the copyeditor who had flagged the problem in the first place, thanking her once again for pointing out the flaws, and saying that the manuscript was going to have to be rewritten. "You wouldn't happen to want to take on some ghostwriting? If not, I can offer you a new manuscript to work on."

That done, she sat back and rubbed her temples. Less than half an hour at work, and she was already exhausted. The day was almost certain to go downhill from here. Time to make another cup of tea—Darjeeling this time, rather than the Earl Grey. Its crispness was just what the day called for.

Tea in hand, she returned to her desk to see whether there were any more fires she had to put out before she could get on with her normal day—making sure everything was on schedule, reviewing copyedited and proofread manuscripts, forwarding invoices so her freelancers would get paid, and so forth. Looking at new manuscripts that had come in had slid down her priority list without Violet around, but she hoped to get to it soon. She also had a couple of manuscripts that she needed to find copyeditors for—and maybe go ahead and line up the indexers now with tentative dates, so they had the time penciled in on their calendars.

Less than half an hour later, Gerri stormed in to interrupt Isobel's work flow. "Are you crazy? You can't accuse him of plagiarism."

"I didn't. I could have, and I have the evidence to back it up—but I didn't. I simply told him that the text needed to be rewritten in his own words and if he doesn't want to do it, he'll have to pay for a ghostwriter to do it."

"That's what we use developmental editors for," Gerri snapped.

"No, it's not." Isobel had had enough. "This isn't a question of rearranging text for logic and smoothing out transitions between ideas, although that's going to need to be done, too. It's a question of him taking three-quarters or more of the book from other sources and just cutting and pasting, with some random paragraphs tacked on with his thoughts about what these other authors meant. It's a mess, where his actual writing is so small it wouldn't even merit a passing grade as a term paper in most classes on this campus. If you want to publish it, even though I've told him twice that it's not publishable, then we need a ghostwriter. Period."

"Why didn't you tell me this before?"

"I did. I rejected his manuscript. I told you there were problems when you handed it to me. I told you about the plagiarism yesterday. You told me to deal with it. This is me dealing."

"Fine. Whatever." Gerri spun to leave. "At least one good thing may come out of this. When I ask for more money in the budget next year, so we can cover unexpected expenses, he's more likely to support the request. Good job." She paused. "In fact, why don't you come to the budget meeting this afternoon? You don't have to say anything, but your presence should remind him that he needs us."

The question was obviously rhetorical, and Gerri left without waiting for a reply. Isobel blew the bangs out of her face. Right, that's why she was doing it—to get a bigger budget for next year. She shook her head and sipped at her

Darjeeling. Whatever had gotten into Gerri since her last vacation, Isobel hoped she got over it soon.

Her next hour of work was uneventful, and she was starting to think today could be productive when the phone rang. She glanced at the Caller ID—Violet!

"Hey, stranger," she said. "You're actually well enough to talk now?"

"A little bit." Violet's laugh turned into a cough. "I was actually calling to thank you for the flowers and see how you're doing. Are things really that bad?"

"And getting worse all the time." Isobel filled Violet in on the current problem manuscript. "Right now, I'm waiting for recommendations and hoping someone has an opening in their schedule."

"Always a problem with the best freelancers," Violet agreed sympathetically. "I hear you had some excitement outside of work yesterday."

"Michael stopped by, did he?"

"Something like that."

Isobel shook her head. She was sure Violet was blushing at the moment—or possibly leering. Isobel didn't want the details.

"I can't believe someone would kill Father Paul," Isobel said. "I mean, I know Sadie was upset with him—she made sure everyone at the Five-and-Diner knew that—but to kill him?"

"It probably wasn't her. Michael said she was out near the college most of the afternoon with her petition."

"Of course not. That would be too easy." Although "most" certainly left some leeway, didn't it? "But who else would do it?" Isobel sighed. "I wish you were here to bounce ideas off. It helped a lot last year."

"You can always talk to Greg," Violet pointed out.

"I'm afraid he'd tell me not to get involved, to let Michael handle everything."

"He didn't last time, did he?"

"Well, no, but last time he was also jealous because he didn't know Michael was my cousin, and yesterday, he did ask whether…" She trailed off into silence for a minute, replaying their conversation in her head. "Oh…he asked if I was going to let Michael solve this one, but he didn't actually say that he wanted me to. I just assumed."

"You know what they say about that."

"Yeah, yeah, yeah. Excuse me—I should call him now."

"Okay. Give him my love. Or at least your love."

Isobel's cheeks heated up. "Talk to you later."

Unfortunately, Greg wasn't answering either his office extension or his cellphone. He did have the one summer session class he was teaching, or he could be at the library, or...She'd call back later.

Meanwhile, it was lunchtime, or near enough that she wouldn't feel guilty about prolonging her break. She didn't even have to head out to the diner today because Momma had taken pity on her and loaded Isobel down with food the night before. "You can't have any of the cookies, but I won't let my only child starve!"

Today, Isobel had brought a simple stew and some rolls to eat with it—not precisely summer fare, but she wasn't about to turn down Momma's cooking. She slid it into the microwave and turned to make herself another cup of tea.

"I've been thinking about our conversation earlier," Gerri said from behind her.

Isobel jumped, knocking over the cup she'd just placed her teabag into. She was glad she hadn't been pouring the boiling water. Her shoulders tensed, and she turned to face her boss. "What about it?"

Gerri stepped inside and closed the door to the hall behind her.

"I think you did the right thing. A good book is good for us—and good for him. And we have to stay on the good side of finance and the Board."

"I didn't know the Board was watching us that closely."

"They're watching everyone. With the current economic climate, they want to trim wherever they can. They could cut our budget—or they could close the press completely." She moued in distaste. "They might even decide to make us a vanity press, where authors have to subsidize their publications."

"I didn't realize it was that bad."

"It might not be, but that's why I took the book in the first place. I figure we need another voice to fight for us in budget meetings, so we need him."

Isobel chewed on her lip. Put like that, she could see Gerri's point. It didn't make the book any better, though. "We still can't afford to pay for the ghostwriter ourselves."

"I know. I talked to him about that, went over our line items, and explained where our discretionary funds actually go—usually to advances for people like him. He understands, he'll pay whatever the going rate is, and he suggested we increase the line item for hiring contractors to cover such contingencies."

Isobel glanced to make certain she wasn't near the water pot, then leaned back against the table. "Sounds good. I've got some requests out, and I should have someone hired within the next couple of days." She felt a burst of sympathy for Gerri, who had been carrying so much worry without sharing it. "Why don't you take off early today? Maybe have Len take you out for a picnic on the town square or something? You could use the break."

Gerri's demeanor froze, and she stared down at the green linoleum. "That's not going to happen."

Isobel frowned. She'd said something wrong. "I thought—"

"He dumped me." Gerri looked up and met Isobel's gaze. Her voice dripped with pain. "At Christmastime, while we were on vacation. He said he'd been planning on it for a while, but he thought he'd give me one last present, a sweet farewell to remember him by. Bastard."

Some farewell.

"I'm sorry."

Gerri brushed off her apology, straightening up and tossing her head back. "It's done now. Get the ghostwriter, get the book fixed, make sure the press doesn't get shut down. And don't forget that budget meeting." She opened the door.

Isobel took a chance and spoke before her boss could leave. "Do I have to go to the meeting? I'm barely coping with my regular work with Violet gone—"

"Speaking of which, when is she going to be back?"

"When the doctor releases her, I imagine," Isobel said. "My point is that I can't really afford to take two or three hours off this afternoon to sit in a meeting where I have no responsibility when I should be here, getting work done."

"The press can't afford for you not to go. We need the money we're asking for. Your new favorite author will remember that if he sees you. Catch up after the meeting."

Favorite. Right. "But won't you and Bill be there?" Bill Regan was the financial officer for the press, and the one who made sure all of her invoices got processed quickly. Isobel didn't want to step on his toes.

"Lots of people bring extras from their department. I'll come by to get you when it's time. Meanwhile, find that ghostwriter." Gerri left.

The Miniature Golf Course Murders

Do everything perfectly and save everyone's jobs. Oh, was that all? It was a good thing Isobel had healthy home-cooked food for lunch; she was going to need her energy this afternoon.

CHAPTER NINE

Thursday, June 17, lunch time

Despite her intentions of focusing on work, Isobel found herself thinking of Momma after she finished her stew. She picked up her second roll and thought of her momma baking the previous day. She had to tell someone, and Greg already knew. Violet probably did too, even if Michael hadn't been present when they had all been discussing it. She called Kimberley.

"Isobel!" Kimberley caroled into the phone. "You found the body without me this time!"

"Is there anyone who doesn't know I found the body?"

"In this town? Don't be silly," Kimberley said. "Don't tell me you were hoping to surprise me with the news."

"I actually wasn't calling about the murder. Momma's planning to open a bakery. At least, I think it's a bakery she has in mind, although she didn't specifically use those words. She just said a shop."

"Isn't it exciting?"

"You knew? Wait…you had to have known. If she's going to sell cookies at Summerfest, she had to get the booth permit from you. You knew, and you didn't tell me?"

"She asked me not to."

Isobel could believe that. Momma had been reluctant to discuss the idea last night and had quickly changed the subject.

Still—"But I'm your best friend! You could have told me."

"Isobel, if my mom asked you not to tell me something, would you tell me anyway?"

The Miniature Golf Course Murders

Isobel made faces at her phone for a few seconds before answering. Why did Kimberley have to sound so reasonable? "I don't know. I suppose it depends on whether I thought you needed to know."

"Exactly. Can you truthfully say you needed to know this? Or did you just *want* to know?"

"It was still a shock. Momma's never seemed interested in working."

"Your mother?" Kimberley chuckled. "One of the women who does her level best to run everything in this town worth running? Involved in every charity, active at church, plays cards with her friends, and keeps an eye on everyone?"

"Exactly! She's already busy with lots of other things."

"And maybe she's busy with all those things because she's trying to fill a hole in her life." Kimberley's voice was soft, and Isobel thought about all Kimberley had done to keep herself busy since John's death the previous year.

"So she's just going to drop all those commitments?"

"I don't know. You'd have to ask her. One thing's for certain, though—she wants to do this, and if you have any sense, you'll support her."

"Of course I will."

"Good. Now, tell me all about finding the body."

Isobel skipped some of the details—the mayor arguing about the election sign, the way the body had looked with the light streaming over her shoulder to highlight the injuries, and even how Brian had thought she'd been pulling a prank on him.

"According to Annie Scott and her friends, the pyramid's a popular make-out spot. Well, not just for making out."

Kimberley laughed. "That hasn't changed. You remember when we used to sneak onto the course?"

"Yes. I was telling Greg about it."

"Well, John and I went without you a few times. I think we might have been the first to use the pyramid."

"Assuming no one else had the same idea."

"We had it first." Kimberley sounded certain. "Anyone else was just copying us."

Isobel didn't point out that John could have been using it with any number of other girls—his apparent fidelity was, they had discovered after his death, a complete sham. "That doesn't explain what Father Paul was doing in it."

"Are you sure?"

Isobel sat still for a moment, processing the thought. Despite her Aunt Rosa's comments about Father Paul being a handsome man, she hadn't considered that he could be unfaithful to his vows of celibacy. After a moment, she said, "I'm sure. He was fully dressed."

"Maybe he was caught before he could get undressed."

"I'm just going to change the topic now."

Kimberley laughed. "Good luck. Everyone's going to talk about the murder. I heard Jim Butler saying he might use 'See the death pyramid' as a new teaser to get people to visit his car lot."

"Tasteful. I hope Richard beats him in the election."

"Are you sure? Jim's wife doesn't strike me as anywhere near as bad as Sue."

"I've put up with Sue this long. I can manage."

After she got off the phone with Kimberley, Isobel checked her e-mail. The copyeditor had declined the chance to try ghostwriting, but a couple of editors had offered to do an introduction via LinkedIn to ghostwriters they knew. She offered the copyeditor her choice of the manuscripts Isobel had on her desk and thanked the editors for the introductions. What else could she get done before Gerri showed back up to drag her off to this budget meeting?

What she really wanted to do was blow off work for the day—especially the budget meeting. She missed the freedom she'd had in December when she took off on a whim to investigate the murders at the Scotts' Christmas tree farm. Then, she'd had Violet to cover the day-to-day routine. Not that "routine" described this day.

Fine, then. She'd worked on what Gerri told her to—getting the ghostwriter—maybe she could squeeze in a little poking around before the meeting. Michael wouldn't have to know. She hesitated. He'd probably find out, and it wasn't like she knew where to start.

All she knew about what Father Paul had done yesterday was that he'd met Sadie for lunch and he'd died at the minigolf course. Michael would be checking on the obvious things—Father Paul's calendar, his to-do list, whether Sadie's time was all accounted for. She should start somewhere else, like the mayor. He'd been at both places as well; he might know something. She was grasping at straws, but she had to start *somewhere*.

By the time she got to City Hall, she'd manufactured an excuse—no, a reason—to talk to the mayor. Isobel suffered through the metal detectors and

The Miniature Golf Course Murders

signing in as a visitor. The last time she'd been in City Hall had been to drive Kimberley home after her bail hearing last year. The cheerful holiday swags and bows had been replaced by cardboard cutouts of suns, pails and shovels, and sunglasses. The swags had looked nicer. She took the stairs to the third floor.

The mayor's office filled the eastern side of the building. His secretary sat at a plain wooden desk directly in front of the carved double doors, the better to block plebeian access, no doubt.

The brunette Daisy Buchanan wannabe at the desk said, "I'm sorry. Mr. Holstein is busy. Would you like to make an appointment and come back? Sometime when you're not out stirring up trouble with innocent bystanders?"

Taken aback, Isobel glanced at the secretary's nameplate—Tara O'Dell. It didn't ring any bells. "Excuse me?"

Tara sneered at her. "You heard me. First you cause trouble for my uncle, then you show up here. Whatever you're after, you're not going to get it."

"Your uncle?"

"Brian O'Dell—at the Minigolf Emporium. You must remember; you were responsible for getting him arrested."

Okay, this wasn't going to be easy. Tara blamed Isobel for Brian's attitude the previous day, didn't want to let Isobel see the mayor, and didn't care whether Isobel thought she was being uncooperative. Isobel decided to focus on what was important to her right now—getting in to see the mayor.

"Odd. I would think in an election year, Richard would make himself more available to voters, rather than less." Isobel gave Tara a wide false smile.

Tara returned the smile in full. "He does. You just need to make an appointment."

"Fine. I'd like an appointment to see him...now."

"You can't do that."

"Is there someone else in there with him now?"

"No."

"Is he out somewhere else?"

"That doesn't matter."

As Isobel opened her mouth to ask whether five minutes would be an acceptable lead time for an appointment, the door opened and Richard stepped out. "I thought I heard voices. Did you need to see me, Isobel?"

"If you have time."

"I should have." He glanced at Tara. "I don't have anything on my schedule right now, do I?" At her mute head shake, he smiled broadly. "Good, good. Come in. What brings you in today?"

Tara shot Isobel a poisonous look, and Isobel knew she didn't have a friend there. Shrugging mentally, she followed Richard into his office and waited for the door to close behind her before she answered his question.

"I was looking at the preparations in the square for Summerfest. It seems they set up the tents earlier every year."

He motioned her to one of the two leather-bound chairs in front of his large desk and leaned against the arm of the other. "Don't tell me. Talk to your friend Kimberley Ansel about that. She has an elaborate timetable all set up so everything is supposed to go without a hitch."

Isobel gave a small laugh. "That sounds like Kimberley. But, no, I wasn't really here to talk about Summerfest—that was just an observation. I was looking around the town square, checking out the shops that line it, that sort of thing."

"The shops love it. They do some great business for Summerfest. This year, I think they're planning to do a sidewalk sale the weekend before and the weekend after, just to see if they can prolong the peak."

"Maybe this weekend, but by the time the festival's over? Most people are going to be all shopped out."

He crossed his arms, and she realized this had probably been his idea. "We'll see, won't we?"

"Yes. It's a pity the Blue Iguana won't be open. This sounds like the sort of experiment Dante would have loved to take part in."

"His displays certainly drew crowds." Richard's tone hadn't thawed any. "Do you know when—or if—he's planning to return?"

The "if" hurt Isobel, but she had to admit it had merit. She had expected Dante to maybe spend a month with his family in California, but he'd gone almost half the year already. "No, his letters are cheerful enough, but he doesn't talk about coming back."

"He writes actual letters? Not e-mail?" He uncrossed his arms and leaned forward.

"Sometimes he sends e-mail, but those tend to be blasts—pictures of what he's been up to, addressed to a dozen people at a time. Mostly, it's actual letters." Because Richard had shown signs of thawing again, Isobel brought up the topic she'd been circling. "I noticed that the Blue Iguana's windows have been papered over, and there are 'Coming Soon' signs up. I know Dante has a ten-year lease, so I was wondering what the realty company's up to. They can't just break the lease like that, can they?"

"I don't know. I'm very sorry, Isobel, but that's not my job. You can ask Dante if he knows what's going on, and maybe if they're breaking the lease, he can sue them, but I can't stop them from doing what they want with their own property."

"Right. Like you didn't stop the McGarritys from putting up that model of the Eiffel Tower made out of beer cans."

"They used cheap beer," he joked.

"But you do have limits on what people can do with their property."

He sighed. "Yes, we do. It's not my job, though, and I'm not the one who insisted the Tower come down. If something violates zoning, you can bring it before the city council and ask them to rule against it, or you can complain directly to the zoning department—which the McGarritys' neighbors did—but I can't be of much use, I'm afraid." He paused. "If that's all, I'm sure Tara has more work lined up for me to do."

Tara probably had nothing of the kind and deliberately tried to keep people from making her boss work, but Isobel refrained from saying so. "Thank you. I'll check into that, then." She stood up. "Wasn't that so terrible yesterday at the minigolf course? Oh, but you left before he was found, didn't you?"

His face smoothed back into the noncommittal mask of a professional politician. "Father Paul's loss is a tragic blow to our community."

"I suppose you don't want your election sign there now. Wouldn't want people connecting you with the murder."

Anger flashed across his face and vanished so quickly Isobel couldn't be certain she'd seen it. "Are you implying something?"

She hadn't thought through what she'd said. Of course he'd take it that way. Isobel shook her head. "Sorry. That wasn't what I meant at all. It's just, you know how voters can be—and the people in this town especially. Every time someone drives past there for the next ten years, they're going to mention the murder."

"Ten?" His face relaxed. "In twenty years, people will be giving directions—'You go east on Main Street, past that old minigolf place where the priest was murdered, then turn...'"

She laughed with him. "True enough. I was just wondering if you wanted that notoriety attached to your campaign."

"I don't know. I may not have much choice. Butler's waging a dirty campaign, and being next to the course might not hurt him. For all I know, he'll use it as a selling point—come to see the murder site, stay to check out the used cars!"

"That's twisted, but Kimberley said the exact same thing." Isobel gave him a sympathetic half-smile. "You know you have my vote. Thanks for taking the time to see me, but you're probably busy and my boss asked me to sit in on a meeting this afternoon."

He shook her hand and led her toward the door. "I appreciate the visit—and the vote. Thanks for coming by."

As the doors closed behind her, Isobel reflected that she didn't know any more about what Richard had done the previous afternoon than she had before. She was out of practice.

CHAPTER TEN

Thursday, June 17, after lunch

Downstairs, she almost collided with her cousin as she stepped out of the elevator. She mock-glared up at him. "Don't you know that exiting passengers have the right of way?"

He ignored her sally. "What are you doing here?"

"I...stopped in to ask who to talk to about Dante's shop. I noticed that someone else is moving in, and I'm sure it's a violation of his lease."

"Did you ask Dante?" Michael's voice dripped with disbelief.

She chewed on her upper lip. That would have been the obvious thing to do.

He stepped in closer, forcing her to strain her neck looking up to meet his eyes. "Leave the investigating to me. We don't want a repeat of last time."

"I wasn't investigating," she protested feebly.

"I know you," he scoffed. "Leave it."

She glowered as he stepped onto the elevator. He did know her, which meant he should know exactly how well telling her *no* would work.

Her fuming continued as she exited the stone building and turned to walk back to her office. Just because it was Michael's job to investigate crimes—and she had more work to do than time to do it in with Violet out sick—and Momma and Aunt Rosa would both disapprove of her getting involved—that didn't mean that she couldn't ask a few questions, did it? She'd tell Michael anything she found out. She'd told him about the poems and the photos last time, hadn't she?

The sunny day made it hard to hold onto her resentment. The town looked festive already, with banners hung from the light posts and fresh flowers in all the planters along the sidewalk. A couple of the shops had sidewalk placards inviting passersby to come in and shop, and most had signs in the window about the upcoming sidewalk sale Richard had mentioned. River Corners Flowers had a little tea caddy in front of their window with small foliage plants on both shelves.

On impulse, Isobel grabbed one of the plants, one that had glossy green leaves with silver spots, and walked in. "Is this easy to care for?"

Sadie looked up from the roses she was stocking in the refrigerated case to one side. "Oh. Isobel." Her voice was chilly. "Yes, all of those that I put out are. It's two ninety-nine plus tax, if you want it."

Isobel dug into her messenger bag and pulled out a five-dollar bill. "I'll take it." She paused. "Should I pay for the flowers I ordered yesterday, while I'm at it?"

Sadie straightened up and walked around the counter to stand at the register. Up close, Isobel could see that Sadie's eyes were red, and she had smudges beneath her eyes where her mascara had smeared. "Let me see…no, the bill's already been sent for that. Kimberley is efficient."

Isobel grinned wryly. "She prides herself on it. Always has. In that case, just the plant." She handed over the cash and waited for her change. "Are you okay?"

Sadie glared at her. "Of course I'm not okay. Why are you all right? Father Paul is dead!"

Flinching from the words, Isobel took a step back before answering. "I think I'm still numb. I'll be a wreck when reality sets in." She knew that from experience. It had taken months for the nightmares to stop after the last dead body, which had been particularly gruesome. This one hadn't been as bloody, but it *was* someone she knew; the emotions were bound to be stronger.

"It's already set in for me." Sadie's voice was bitter. "I was angry at him, but I didn't want him dead. And now I can't—we can't—I'll never be able to say I'm sorry for yelling at him like that in public, you know? What kind of monster could kill someone like that, could kill him? Why?"

Isobel didn't point out that people killed each other all the time, sometimes for very trivial reasons. She couldn't imagine anyone having a good motive to kill Father Paul. He'd always been open and caring, and when the scandals about priests in the Catholic Church first started coming to light, he was among the voices calling for those priests to be removed from their priestly duties and prosecuted, just as they would be for any other crime.

Rather than saying any of that, Isobel said, "I'm sure the police will figure it out."

Sadie nodded absently. She pointed at the plant. "Give it indirect light, and make sure you don't overwater it. Once a week is plenty."

"Thanks." Sadie found herself standing out on the sidewalk with a plant she didn't know what to do with and more questions than she'd had when she left her office. Her two best leads—Sadie, who had been angry enough at Father Paul to start a petition against him, and Richard, who as far as Isobel knew had no grudge but had been in the right place at the right time—had come to nothing. Maybe Michael was right and she should stick to her own work. She certainly had enough of it on her plate.

First, though, there were workers in powder-blue overalls in front of the Blue Iguana on the south side of the square, unloading boxes from the back of a double-parked delivery truck. Maybe they knew what was going on, why Dante's shop was being remodeled.

She crossed the street and strolled past the other businesses open for business—lingerie, beads, books—all the boutiques an arty college town could want. The Blue Iguana, however, stood out as a hive of activity on the block.

Brown paper covered the plate windows, and she couldn't see inside. Sounds of hammers and power tools chased each other out the open front door of the shop, and men and women went back and forth between the shop and the truck. When she reached the Blue Iguana, she stood and waited for one of the workers to notice her. A pair went by with a large box on a dolly—one pushing, the other calling out directions.

Another called up into the back of the truck. "No, not that one next. The one marked 3A. If we don't put them in in the right order, it's harder." He nodded at Isobel but turned back to make sure the workers in the truck were doing what he'd said.

Voices came from the open door of the shop. "Hey, this isn't going to fit here." "Sure it will." "Look at the plan, you idiots. You're on the wrong wall."

She stepped closer to the truck. "Remodeling?"

"Mm-hmm." He didn't look at her.

"I thought the Blue Iguana still had the lease on this place."

"Yeah, the guy that owns the Iguana has cancer, decided to close it up permanently. He's sublet it."

Permanently? Well, Dante had said it would stay closed when he came back to town, but she hadn't realized he meant forever. Still…"Sublet? To whom?"

Now he did look at her. "You'll just have to wait and see the new shop when it opens, like everyone else."

"Sounds like a state secret!"

He laughed. "No, those get leaked to the press. This one? We're just getting paid to do the work." He glanced back up into the truck. "You got the right one this time, Fred? All right, then, get going so we can get the truck emptied before that meter maid comes back."

"Thanks." She walked past, trying to catch a glimpse of the remodeling inside through the open door, but all she saw was bare wood studs with wallboard leaning against it. Whatever the workers were installing, it wasn't where she could see it.

Back at her office, she reflected that all she had to show for her exertions this afternoon was a new plant. She stared around the office and decided to set it on the table with the hotpot and her tea supplies, where she'd be more likely to remember to water it. Then she opened the lower drawer of her desk and dropped her messenger bag inside. Time to get back to work, before Gerri showed up to drag her off to this meeting.

One of the ghostwriters on LinkedIn had sent her a message, saying he appreciated the introduction, but he was booked solid for the next six months. Fortunately, the other had better news. "The schedule slipped on one of my books—contract issues. That means I might be able to fit your job in, depending on the scope of the project." Isobel sent a brief message about what she had and what she needed. She ended by asking, "Would six weeks be sufficient time to address this? If so, I'll e-mail you the file and a W-9 for you to fill out."

That was one major worry off her list. Quickly, she sent e-mails to indexers, asking for time penciled in later in the summer, as well as to copyeditors for the other projects she had on hand. Now she could go to the meeting with a mostly clean conscience, at least as far as getting work accomplished for the day.

She still had some time, however, so she opened a new e-mail message. Dante didn't like e-mail much, as she'd told Richard, but this gave her time to make sure she had the wording right, which made e-mail better than a phone call—and quicker than a standard letter.

"I hear you've sublet the Iguana. Who could possibly take your place downtown?"

She hesitated but decided not to directly ask him whether he was coming back to River Corners. She missed him, but he needed to do what was best for him. She knew that. She sent the e-mail and moved on to vendor requests, the next item on her to-do list. That should keep her occupied until Gerri showed up!

CHAPTER ELEVEN

Thursday, June 17, evening

After the meeting, Isobel wanted nothing more than to go home, fill her tub with chamomile and valerian, and fall asleep relaxing. Ralf Enzian, author of the most problematic manuscript ever, had been every bit as unpleasant and condescending as she'd expected, but Gerri seemed oblivious to his tone. Then the meeting itself had gone on forever, with Power Point presentations and handouts full of numbers and long digressive arguments about historic uses of funds and whether earmarked items ought to be reconsidered.

Instead of heading to the comfort of her cottage, however, she brewed herself a cup of Earl Grey tea and sat down at her desk, aiming to at least get her inbox cleared before she left for the day. That had to be doable, right? First, though, the light on her phone was blinking, which meant at least one voice mail.

She'd missed a call from Greg while she was in the meeting. Suppressing a sigh, she listened to his message. "Sorry I was out. I'm trying to get everything packed so I can move as soon as I find a place. I'm sort of afraid I'll wind up stashing the boxes in the department storeroom and sleeping on the office floor. We're still on for Saturday, right?"

She sipped her tea before calling him back. He answered on the second ring. "Hey, you."

"Hey. Did you want help packing? I can drop by for a bit after I get my e-mail tamed." She sighed as the mail program dinged, announcing more new messages to deal with. "Or after I just decide to surrender to the inevitable."

His voice was husky. "I don't think we'd get much packing done."

"Mmmm. Sounds much better than e-mail."

"Definitely. But I do want to get the boxes packed. Saturday?"

"Yes, I'm still coming with you on Saturday. Gives me something to look forward to while I slog through these new meetings Gerri's insisting on and budget woes and plagiarism crises and…"

"Breathe," he said. "You can only do one thing at a time. Focus on the e-mail for now. Only one more day to get through this week. You can do it."

"I hope so. The Japanese have a word for dying of overwork, you know."

He laughed. "One more day. I promise you don't have to work on Saturday."

"I'll hold you to that."

The one bright spot in her e-mail was a faster-than-expected reply from Dante. "You say the sweetest things, but I'll bet you're in there oftener even than you came to visit me! Also, I have a surprise for you—I think you'll like it. Mom says to tell you hello."

Curiouser and curiouser. She typed out an answer. "This surprise better be worth it, and somehow I doubt there could be anywhere I'd shop more often—I don't even hit the Five-and-Diner as often as I used to, hard as that may be to believe."

She then proceeded to catch him up on Father Paul's death. "I'm sure Michael thinks I found him on purpose, and of course he doesn't want me to have anything to do with it. I'm happy to leave it to him this time; I've enough on my plate as it is."

Perhaps *happy* wasn't the best word for it, but if she told herself that often enough, she might believe it. She'd enjoyed poking around last December and figuring out what was going on. She hadn't enjoyed Jennifer's visit to her office much, that was true, but Isobel had had the satisfaction of figuring out who the killer was. However, she had told Greg that she'd leave the investigating to Michael this time.

Except…she had been poking around at the mayor's office, hadn't she? And Michael had even caught her there. She sighed. She might as well come clean with Dante.

The last sentence became "I should be happy to leave it to him this time; I've enough on my plate as it is." She thought for a moment, then added, "Somehow, though, I found myself poking around at lunchtime. If you hear that he's thrown me in jail for interfering with an investigation, it's because I couldn't help myself."

After that, the e-mail went quickly, and she left work only an hour later than usual. She stretched as she walked out into the sunshine. What should she do with herself? Greg was busy, and her momma was probably baking more cookies for the festival. She probably had hundreds of cookies already, but for five days of sales? Momma was going to try for thousands, if Isobel knew her. Momma might welcome some help, but she might also get upset with Isobel for going to talk to Richard today. Better to avoid her for now.

A whole evening to herself! She should probably have brought manuscripts home to read, but she'd put in enough hours for one day. A nice light yoga routine, followed by a relaxing soak in the tub with one of the books from her tottering to-be-read pile, seemed like just the thing.

Windows were open in Kimberley's house, but no sound came from inside. Because it was summer, there were no lights either, so no way to tell whether or not Kimberley was home. Where else would she be? She might be working on preparing for Summerfest, but she was as likely to do that at home as in her office.

Isobel paused next to the side door, debating whether to knock. She and Kimberley used to stay up until all hours, talking about everything and nothing—and even after Kimberley and John had gotten married, Isobel often dropped in on the spur of the moment. She hadn't done it as often over the past few months—because she was seeing Greg and didn't have as much time? Or because Kimberley was widowed, which left Isobel uncomfortable talking about all the things the three of them—plus Dante—had done together growing up? Or because Kimberley had thrown herself even more enthusiastically into her work, keeping herself busy all the time? Maybe a little of all three.

She really should make time to talk to her friend—not that Kimberley had seemed down when they chatted on the phone, but just because they were friends. Not tonight, though. With Isobel's extra workload, she really wanted the relaxing evening before going back to face Gerri and plagiarism and vendors and everything else tomorrow morning. Maybe when Violet got back to work, Isobel could relax a little, and Kimberley would be done with Summerfest, so they could just have a girls' night.

It was time for that chamomile and valerian tub—and if Isobel felt just a little lonely and morose, it was just because she was tired and overworked, right? At least this time, no one had broken into her cottage.

CHAPTER TWELVE

Friday, June 18, evening

Aunt Rosa's house was as different from her sister's as it was possible to be. Where Momma put on a public face of delicacy that fooled no one who knew her, Aunt Rosa was straightforward. Her living room had sofa and chairs that, if not the latest fashion, were only a few years from the furniture store's showroom. Her home was completely conventional, absolutely comfortable, and simply charming.

Isobel nodded Greg toward a chair. "Why don't you catch the news, or the baseball game, or whatever's got my cousin so enthralled? I'm going to go say hello to Aunt Rosa."

Greg said, "Are you sure? I can set the table."

Michael glanced up. "You're late. She had me set it half an hour ago."

"We are not late. This is the same time I always get here," Isobel protested.

"Maybe you're always late, and we're too polite to have told you."

"You, polite? That'll be the day."

In the kitchen, Momma was tossing a salad while Aunt Rosa sliced a roast. Isobel kissed both their cheeks before asking, "Is there something I can do to help?"

"You could make the gravy," her momma said.

Isobel sighed. "Momma, I can't. You remember what happened last time."

"Very well," Momma said. "If you don't want more practice before Thanksgiving. I can just imagine how your gravy will turn out then, with the last time you made it months prior."

Isobel looked at Aunt Rosa, who carefully didn't meet her gaze. So much for her aunt taking her side. "I don't know where the flour is," she muttered.

Momma was unsympathetic. "Everything you need is by the stove. Start with the pan drippings."

That much, she remembered. Aunt Rosa had used a metal roasting pan, so Isobel turned on the burner it rested on. A full set of measuring cups sat next to the canister of flour. Isobel thought furiously—how much flour was she supposed to use? Momma had told her something about ratios of fat to binding and liquid, and how all the sauces were based on the same idea, but all Isobel could remember was that she'd goofed and added the flour to the pan before the butter, and the smoke had taken hours to clear out of the kitchen.

She took a deep breath. That wasn't going to be an issue this time; the drippings were in the pan. She wouldn't burn anything. Deciding to err on the side of caution, she grabbed the quarter-cup measuring cup and scooped flour into the pan before using a whisk to stir it in. The aroma rising from the pan owed everything to her Aunt Rosa, Isobel knew, but it helped her feel better anyway. The reddish-brown liquid (Aunt Rosa must have used some wine to cook the roast with) still looked rather watery, so Isobel added more flour and watched in horror as the liquid bound up and stuck into globs around the edge of the pan.

"Help!"

Momma shook her head from the other side of the room. "You're doing fine. Add your liquid."

This wasn't fair. She hadn't expected to have to cook tonight. Michael was going to pronounce the gravy inedible, and Greg would know that she was hopeless, and Aunt Rosa would laugh at Momma for thinking she could teach someone else to cook, and—

A whiff of smoke reached her. She grabbed the cup of water next to the stove and dumped it in left-handed while frantically whisking with her right. To her amazement, the gravy—because it was gravy now—started to smooth out, although it still looked too thick.

She crossed to the sink and refilled the cup. This time, she added the water a little at a time, still mixing. The gravy blooped and blopped, and some splattered onto the base of her thumb. She quickly stuck her hand in her mouth to ease the pain and was surprised at how good the gravy tasted.

"That's no way to treat a burn," Aunt Rosa said.

"I know, I know." Isobel turned off the burner and shifted the roaster away from the heat, then went to the sink to run cold water over her hand, but she didn't really care about the burn. She had made gravy!

"You have to hear this!" Greg called from the living room.

Isobel turned off the water, wrapped a towel around her hand, and went to see what had caught his attention.

Michael had paused the TV, and as Isobel came in, trailed by Momma and Aunt Rosa, he turned the volume up.

It was a political commercial—and one that was hastily put together, judging by its content. Jim Butler stood in front of the building on his used car lot. "River Corners deserves truth and justice. Richard Holstein was seen at the site of a murder. We need to know why. We deserve answers. And River Corners deserves a mayor who isn't a suspect in a murder investigation. Remember this on election day. I am Jim Butler, and I approve this message."

"That was quick," Isobel said. "How'd he get them to air it so fast?"

"If he'd already paid for the spot, they probably wouldn't care if he switched out the clip," Greg said. "Is he right, though—is the mayor a suspect?"

"Everyone's a suspect, even you," Michael said.

Isobel said, "I wouldn't hit someone over the head!"

"No, I think we've already established that you'd poison them."

"Oh, that reminds me—I made the gravy tonight."

Michael opened his mouth to say something, glanced behind her at their mothers, and shut his mouth.

Greg grinned. "Is it time to eat, then?"

"You boys can put the food on the table," Aunt Rosa said. "And if someone drops the gravy on the floor, you won't get anything to eat."

"Drat. There went my next line of defense," Michael said, standing. "Maybe I should go on a fast."

Once they were all seated at the table—Michael sitting as conspicuously far from the gravy as possible—Aunt Rosa said a blessing for the food, adding at the end, "And please bless the soul of your servant Father Paul, taken from this Earth too soon."

"Amen."

Food was passed, and plates were filled. Greg poured gravy all over his roast, and even Michael put some on his mashed potatoes. Isobel lifted her fork and hesitated for just a second before biting into it herself. She could make chili. Surely simple gravy wasn't beyond her? Besides, she'd already tasted it.

She relaxed and began enjoying the meal.

"Rosa," Momma said, "This roast isn't bad at all. Not as good as I could do, of course, but not bad."

"Why Maria Elena, how sweet. Especially when you worked so hard to open those bags of lettuce to make the salad."

Isobel hid her smile behind a forkful of potatoes. Across the table, Greg winked at her.

"I suppose the commercial could have been worse," Isobel said. "He could've said that the police chief had questioned the mayor already."

Michael glared at her, but his mouth was full, so Momma spoke before he could. "And just how would you know that?"

"I saw him there." Too late, Isobel realized she was admitting to snooping.

"Did you now?" Momma stabbed at her salad. "It must be nice to have free time on your hands. And to not worry about whether a murderer is going to come after you again when you're alone."

"It was the middle of the day in City Hall," Isobel protested. "No one's alone there. And they make visitors sign in and everything—if I didn't sign out, there would have been problems."

"She called me first," Greg added. He didn't mention that he hadn't picked up the phone, implying that he knew where she was and why. She flashed him a smile of thanks for the support.

"Which doesn't mean she couldn't have been in danger after she left the building." Michael had finally finished the food in his mouth. "Isobel, I know you're curious. I know your help was crucial in solving Laurie and John's murders. I also know that no one at this table wants anything to happen to you. Please stay out of it this time and let me do my job."

Isobel stared down at her plate. She just wanted to help—and she was the one who found the dead body this time. He wouldn't even know about it if it weren't for her. Instead of answering him, she ate another forkful of potatoes.

After a minute of uncomfortable silence as everyone waited for Isobel to say something and she made it clear that she wasn't going to, Aunt Rosa said, "I think that's quite enough talk about murder for one evening. It's enough to put someone off their appetite."

The Miniature Golf Course Murders

The empty serving dishes scattered around the table gave the lie to her comment, but no one said so. No one would have dared.

Momma spoke up. "What about Mass on Sunday? Who's going to be taking the nine o'clock now? Not Father Terrence?"

Aunt Rosa shook her head. "Not this week. I heard the bishop's coming down. Of course, with the priest shortage in the diocese, Father Terrence probably will have to serve by himself for a while."

"Pity. Father Terrence is so inexperienced."

"That he is." Aunt Rosa raised her fork to point at Michael. "I don't want to hear any excuses from you this week. You're not too busy to go to church when the bishop's in town."

Michael rolled his eyes. "Ma—"

"Don't you 'Ma' me, either. You be there."

"Yes, Ma."

Silence reined for a few more minutes as everyone gave their attention to the food.

Finally, Greg pushed his plate away. "Please tell me there's no dessert. I don't think I could eat another bite."

"Well, it's not my sister's *cookies*, but I did bake a strawberry-rhubarb pie," Aunt Rosa said. "It's not as if I had anything better to do with myself, since she didn't ask me to help her."

"She didn't ask me to help, either," Isobel quickly interjected, trying to forestall another argument.

"Thank God for that," Michael said. "For the sake of the town."

Momma had started to look defensive when Aunt Rosa was talking, but now her mouth pinched closed and her eyebrows came down. "That will be quite enough out of you about my daughter's cooking. I don't notice you keeling over on the floor—and I think that's your third serving of gravy this evening."

"Fourth," Greg chipped in helpfully.

Isobel raised her eyebrows at her cousin, and he shrugged. "Still doesn't mean I want to eat any cookies you make. She'd probably wind up using rotten eggs or something."

"I know what rotten eggs smell like," Isobel said. "Sort of like the inside of your car."

He started to retort, but his mother cut him off. "None of which addresses why my sister didn't even ask if I'd be interested in helping."

"I didn't think you'd want to," Momma said. "Besides…"

"Yes?"

"I wanted to do this for me, and if anyone else knew you were involved, it wouldn't be mine any more."

"That's ridiculous. No one would care."

"I would. But then, that wouldn't matter to you, would it?" Momma stood up. "Enjoy your pie. Isobel, don't forget you promised to come over tomorrow evening."

CHAPTER THIRTEEN

Saturday, June 19, early morning

Isobel had just rinsed her teacup in the sink when Greg knocked on her door and stepped inside. "I see you're not worried enough to lock your door."

"I unlocked it about ten minutes ago because I knew you were going to be here." She glanced at the clock. "I wasn't expecting you quite this early, though. I was thinking about baking some cinnamon rolls."

"Pillsbury?"

"No, from scratch."

"How about I take you out for breakfast instead? There's a cute little place north of town I've been meaning to try, and I made reservations."

"The Farmhouse? I've heard good things about it." Mostly from the proprietors, who had been high school classmates of her and Kimberley.

She grabbed her messenger bag and locked the door behind her. Greg had parked his car next to hers, and she slid into the passenger seat. "I can make cinnamon rolls, you know. I even have the dough all refrigerated."

He leaned across and kissed her. "I believe you. This is just a thank-you for coming with me."

Slightly mollified, she fastened her seatbelt. She'd have to bake the rolls before the dough went bad, though. Maybe she could bake them Monday and take them in to work, use the sugar to help keep her focused. Because that always worked. Mentally, she stuck out her tongue at herself.

Half a mile north of town, K & B's Farmhouse had a gravel lot already packed with cars despite the early hour. A few tables graced the wrap-around porch of the pale yellow house, and more spread across the tan brick patio behind. Isobel tucked her hand into Greg's and followed him up the wooden steps to the screened front door.

As Greg reached for the screen door, it was pushed open from the inside. "Excuse me."

Isobel stepped back to avoid the door and glanced at the man holding it—her problem author from the college. At least he was leaving. "Mr. Enzian! What a surprise."

He drew his heavy eyebrows together. "Do I know you?"

She forced a smile. "We met at the budget meeting yesterday? Gerri Hess introduced us."

"Ah, yes." If anything, his frown grew deeper. "The young lady who doesn't like the way I wrote my book."

She pinched her lips together. Opening her mouth would only lead to words coming out that shouldn't, such as if he'd actually written the book rather than copying it from several different people, it wouldn't be a problem.

Fortunately, he didn't seem to expect a response, brushing past them without another word. Greg motioned Isobel toward the door, and she went in.

Inside, the house had been remodeled—gutted—to make it more airy, with white-washed posts providing support instead of interior walls. The kitchen was still separate from the eating area, but swinging shutters replaced the solid door that had divided it in the past. The only table not occupied was next to the far windows. A paper tent labeled RESERVED sat in front of the vase with bachelor's buttons and red and white carnations.

A blonde waitress rushing by said, "I'll be back to get your name in a minute, but it's at least a half an hour wait."

"I have a reservation," Greg said.

"Oh! Okay, in that case, someone will be right with you." She vanished through the swinging shutters.

"Right with you" translated to about five minutes later, as servers brought food to tables, refilled coffee, tea, and juice glasses, and thanked people again for coming. A table with young children became the center of attention as cereal flew everywhere and the girl started shrieking, "He got Ginger wet!"

The same waitress passed by again, saying, "Sorry about this. Families usually come in later." She didn't wait for an answer, rushing off to deal with the table.

A man in a white chef's jacket stepped out of the kitchen. Isobel waved, and he grinned, came over, and enveloped her in a hug. "Isobel! You should have told us you were coming. There's a wait."

Isobel motioned at Greg. "He made a reservation." She added, "Greg, this is Ben, the titular B of the Farmhouse. We went to school together. Ben, this is Greg. He works at the college."

"No doubt where the two of you met." Ben shook Greg's hand. "Pleased to meet you. Here, I'll show you to your table, and as soon as Chrissy's finished dealing with the disaster of the hour, she'll be over to get you something to drink."

Isobel and Greg fell into step behind Ben, who kept half-turning around to keep tabs on them. Isobel said, "Actually, we met at the Blue Iguana. He ducked in to get out of a snowstorm."

Ben's face fell. "Too bad about the Blue Iguana closing."

He paused, as they had reached the table, and the three of them stood there for a moment.

Isobel nodded. "I saw something else going in already."

"Already? It's been closed for months," Greg said.

Isobel and Ben both looked at him for a minute, then turned back to face each other. Ben said, "Yes. I know there were a couple of ovens delivered the other day."

"Ovens? More competition for you?"

"We'll see." Ben waved them to the chairs. "I have to get back to work. Let me know next time when you're coming, and we'll do something special."

Greg watched him leave, a slight frown on his face. "Another of your high school conquests?"

She giggled. "He hung around a lot, but in retrospect, I think he was after Dante."

"He certainly seemed pleased to see you."

"He and Ken have been talking about opening a restaurant for years. I promised them that when they did, I'd come."

"You could have said something. We could've come months ago."

"I don't know why I didn't." She shrugged. "It just never seemed to come up when we were together." She stared down at her silverware. "And Momma always says the woman shouldn't be planning the dates."

He shook his head in exasperation. "Has it ever occurred to you that your momma doesn't live in this century?"

"Frequently. However, I haven't figured out a way to silence this voice in my head."

Greg reached across and took her hand in his. "You don't have to silence it. Just, maybe, argue back occasionally. And the next time you want to go somewhere or try something, let me know. I promise I won't run away."

Tears prickled at her eyes. He knew that was a sore spot for her; she still didn't know where her dad had gotten to when he'd left in the middle of the night. She wanted to tell him not to make promises he couldn't keep, but instead, she nodded silently.

"Hi, I'm Chrissy, and I'll be your server this morning, barring more unexpected drama." The blonde stood next to their table, a pad in her hand. "Can I get you some drinks to start off?" She blinked. "Hey, aren't you two the ones who found the body? I'm so glad we didn't stop in the pyramid! Ron wanted to—said that Annie and Frank could go on ahead—but I just wanted to play, and…sorry. I'm babbling. Can I get you those drinks?"

Isobel said, "I'll have some hot tea."

"What kind would you like? We have orange, Earl Grey, English breakfast, Russian caravan, oolong—"

Isobel interrupted. "The English breakfast will be fine for now. I might want to try some of the orange later."

Chrissy grinned at her. "We sell packets of it, so if you want, you can buy some to take with you."

"I'll keep that in mind."

Greg said, "I'll have some coffee, please. Black, no sugar. And some orange juice with breakfast."

"Got it. I'll get those right out to you." She closed the pad, slipped it into her apron pocket, and left.

"That's who we are for the foreseeable future, you know," Isobel said. "The two who found the body."

"Would anyone care if I told them I was just standing outside?"

"Probably not." She squeezed his hand. "Do you think she'll remember to bring us menus when she brings our drinks?"

"Probably not."

The view out the window was a cottage-style garden, with informal beds of flowers crowded together. Gravel paths broke up the beds, and a bench sat in the shade of a weeping cherry, which must have been magnificent in the spring. Taller bushes formed hedges that screened this section of the garden from the road and from the rest of the property. Tops of heads hinted at other garden retreats beyond the one that they could see.

"Looks like a pleasant place to wait if you don't have a reservation."

Greg waggled his eyebrows at her. "Sure, if you don't mind everyone in the restaurant seeing how you pass the time."

Her cheeks heated up, and she glanced down at their hands.

"I have a confession to make." Greg sounded serious, and Isobel looked up in alarm. "I did some snooping by the minigolf course yesterday when I was supposed to be thinking about next year's classes."

"Oh, really? And you didn't take me along?"

"I figured one of us should be working—and I don't think your boss likes me much."

"Right now, I don't think she likes the world much. However, your tact is appreciated." She leaned her chin on the hand he wasn't holding. "Are you going to tell me what you found?"

"I thought you said you were going to let Michael investigate this one." His eyes danced with amusement behind his glasses.

She stuck out her tongue at him. "*I* thought you wanted me to say that because you didn't want to have to rescue me again."

His tone was warm and serious. "I've never met anyone less like a damsel in distress."

"So you won't mind if I poke around? Or tell my cousin?"

"As long as we're doing it together."

She smiled. "Agreed. Are you going to tell me what you found?" she repeated.

Just then, Chrissy arrived carrying a tray that held two cups, a pot of hot water for the tea, sachets of tea, and a carafe of coffee. Greg released Isobel's hand, and they both leaned back slightly to give Chrissy more room.

"Now, what can I get you?" The pad was back in Chrissy's hand.

"Some menus, perhaps?" Greg said.

Chrissy flushed, and Isobel winced in sympathy. The teen's morning—at least what she'd seen of it—was definitely on the hectic side. Besides, Ben really ought to have given them the menus when he seated them.

Chrissy took a step back, ready to fetch the menus, and Isobel reached out. "No, wait. What are today's specials?"

"There's a spicy hash with chorizo, mixed peppers, and gold and blue potatoes; a seasonal omelet—I'll have to double-check that we haven't run out of the vegetable mix; and sweet potato pancakes with berries and cream."

Isobel glanced at Greg, eyebrows raised. He looked from her to Chrissy and said, "I'll try the hash. That sounds good. Can I get it with a couple of eggs on the side, sunny-side up?"

Chrissy smiled in relief and pulled the pad back out. "And for you?" she asked Isobel.

"They all sound good, but—does Ken still make those layered eggs?"

"He might." Chrissy looked doubtful. "But he's not working today. I can get you a menu, if you want."

Isobel shook her head. "Just tell Ben to surprise me."

After Chrissy had left, Greg said, "That is one problem with being in academia. You don't always get a position close to home. You've known these people all your life, you rent a cottage from your best friend—and I can't even remember the last time I saw *my* best friend. It can be hard, putting down new roots."

"You could take a vacation, go back home to visit."

He shook his head. "Maybe next year. This year's a little too busy, with André coming in to take John's place next year, and gearing up for the search for a more permanent replacement. Plus moving house, of course."

"Of course. You said John's place—isn't Petersen getting replaced, too?"

He grimaced. "Not yet. He's got tenure, so until he's actually convicted, the college is leaving him in place. I think it's just to save themselves the expense of another lawsuit, but it probably means we'll be going through this again in a couple of years, once his trial is settled one way or the other."

"That's annoying."

"It could be worse. You'll note I said *another* lawsuit. Jennifer is suing the college for wrongful termination."

"You're kidding."

"Nope." He sipped his coffee and nodded approvingly. "It seems she thinks they shouldn't be able to fire her 'for cause' until she's been found guilty."

"She doesn't have tenure, though. She's only been here a little longer than you, right?" Isobel shook her head. "That doesn't make any sense."

"In case you hadn't noticed, Jennifer has a huge sense of entitlement."

Isobel had noticed. When she'd first met the other woman, Isobel had thought Jennifer felt entitled to Greg. That hadn't been who she was after, but Isobel still didn't like Jennifer or feel any sympathy for her.

"I hope the judge throws the case out of court. Now, then," she said, leaning forward, "are you going to tell me what you found at the minigolf course or not?"

CHAPTER FOURTEEN

Saturday, June 19, breakfast

Greg chuckled. "I could wait and see if we're going to get interrupted again."

"Don't you dare."

"All right, all right." He leaned in and dropped his voice. No doubt others in the restaurant thought he was whispering sweet nothings to her. In her opinion, this was far better—at least right now. "As I drove by, I saw some kids ducking out of a hole in the fence on the side facing the car lot. I couldn't see where they went because of the trees and the ditch there."

"A hole in the fence beats trying to climb it," Isobel said. "But if that's true, the killer could be anyone—someone who walked in the front door, or someone who slipped in from outside." She groaned. "At least when there was a limited suspect pool, I thought this case might wrap up quickly. Now,…"

"It could be anyone." He sipped at his coffee again. "This case wasn't going to wrap up quickly, though. It's already been a couple of days, and Michael hasn't made an arrest or even brought people in for questioning—except for the course manager, that is."

"Oh, is Brian the manager?"

Greg fished a business card out of his wallet. "I grabbed this before we left the other day. Brian O'Dell, general manager. It's got the Website address and his e-mail, too."

"I don't think Michael would be too happy if I started e-mailing his suspects." Isobel fingered the card. "At least I'm assuming Brian's a suspect."

"Everyone's a suspect," Greg said. "Except possibly you."

"That's only because if he arrested me, Momma and Aunt Rosa wouldn't let him hear the end of it."

"Perfect! You can commit a murder and know that you'll get away scot-free."

She grinned evilly. "I should put together a little list."

"Who'd none of them be missed?"

"No, they'd none of them be missed."

Their laughter was interrupted by Chrissy's arrival with their food. "Your hash." She set it down in front of Greg. "Be careful. The plate's hot." She turned to Isobel and set down another plate. "He said he'd come out to see what you think."

"Thank you." Isobel said, staring at the plate in front of her, which had a Belgian waffle topped with sweet potatoes, onions, and wilted greens, with fried eggs placed on the top. It wasn't quite Ken's layered eggs, but it looked fabulous.

"Can I get you anything else? More hot water? Juice?"

"I wanted orange juice," Greg reminded her.

Isobel sighed and indicated her hot water pot. "Could you heat that up for me, please? I forgot to brew my tea."

"Sure thing. I'll be right back with those for you."

"That's one of your more endearing traits, you know."

Isobel looked at Greg, puzzled. "What is?"

"You're so detail oriented in your work. You can track down clues and solve murders. Yet you are absolutely absent-minded when it comes to your food and drink."

"It's one of the reasons I'm a bad cook," Isobel said. "It doesn't do to be absent-minded in the kitchen."

"The gravy the other day was fine. A little lumpy, perhaps—"

"Augh!" She banged the palm of her hand into her forehead. "I forgot to strain it. I'm terrified of what I might forget to do with the turkey."

"As long as it's cooked, everyone will eat it. No one makes a perfect turkey every year," he reassured her.

"Do yourself a favor. Don't say that in front of Momma." Isobel cut the corner off her waffle, making sure that she had sweet potato, greens, and egg white on her fork as well. She chewed thoughtfully. "It's not just spinach. I wonder if he'd be willing to tell me what else is in there."

"Are you going to try cooking it yourself?" Greg teased.

"Maybe just the potatoes and greens." She winked at him. "Don't worry, I wouldn't ask you to eat it yet."

He shrugged. "I trust you. Mostly."

Isobel pointed her fork at his plate. "Eat. Before that gets cold." She took another forkful of waffle. "And then we can get back to speculating about the murder. What I still can't understand is why Father Paul agreed to meet someone there in the first place."

"Maybe he was blackmailing someone with something he heard in the confessional?"

"He couldn't do that. If he heard a confession, that's between him, the penitent, and God."

"What if the penitent told him about something someone else had done?" Greg ate a bite of the chorizo. "Mmm. Spicy. He could talk to that other person, couldn't he?"

"Maybe." Isobel wasn't sure where the boundaries of secrecy were. She'd certainly complained about her momma's over-bearing attitude often enough when she was a teenager. She didn't want to think that could have gotten back to Momma.

"Here's your drinks," Chrissy said. She looked at Isobel. "What do you think?"

"It's delicious. I don't suppose he'd be willing to tell me what's in it besides the spinach?"

"I'll ask." Chrissy seemed pleased. "You know, no one's ever ordered off-menu before. I think he liked the challenge."

A howl from one of the toddlers made them all look around. Chrissy sighed. "As opposed to the challenges I face. I'll let him know you like it." She headed off to the family's table once again.

Isobel set her fork down and placed two tea sachets in her teapot. Trust Ben and Ken to use loose-leaf teas rather than bagged ones that were so often full of tea dust.

"I wonder whether Michael knows why Father Paul was there."

"If he does, would he tell you?" Greg asked. "I get the feeling he's not nearly as understanding about your streak of curiosity."

"It depends on whether he thought I'd go poking around somewhere dangerous if he didn't tell me, trying to find out on my own. Odds are, he doesn't think the church is all that dangerous." She reached toward his plate with her fork. "Can I try some?"

"Sure. I hadn't expected the blue potatoes to look so...purple."

Isobel laughed and speared some of the offending tubers. She popped them into her mouth. "Oooh. Buttery. Very yummy—no matter what color they are. Did you want to try some of the waffle?"

"I'll pass this time. I think this is more than enough to fill me up."

"Good thing we're going to be walking around. Otherwise, I might fall asleep."

"I'll make sure to have the air-conditioning going in the car."

They ate for a couple minutes in silence, enjoying their food. Then, "They had forensics going over the pyramid, right?" Greg said thoughtfully.

"Yes, but it sounds like fingerprints are going to be a nightmare." Isobel peeked at her tea, decided it looked strong enough, and pulled out the sachets.

"They could get more information than that, though. Like whether the person was taller than Father Paul, if he was hit from in front or behind, that sort of thing."

"I can tell you right now that the person was not likely to be taller than Father Paul, as the only two people I know in that category are you and Michael."

"There goes that lead," he said cheerfully.

"I'll keep my ears open at Mass tomorrow," Isobel said. "I'll probably mostly hear gossip, but there might be something useful. And we can see if Michael's willing to share any information at dinner. Aunt Rosa and Momma are both bound to be full of questions."

"Such a useful pair!" Greg looked up. "Your boyfriend's coming."

Isobel looked over to see Ben making his way across the room. "I told you, he was after Dante," she said softly.

"I can't see it myself."

She would have said more, but Ben had reached the table. "Chrissy said you like it? I've been toying with putting it on the menu, but I wasn't sure anyone would eat it."

"I love it," Isobel said honestly. "I could almost see it with fried chicken mixed in, but it's delicious. What greens did you use besides spinach?"

"Mixed greens—we grow them out back." Ben looked thoughtful. "I hadn't thought about chicken. Are you sure that wouldn't be too much food?"

She laughed. "It looks like all your plates are too much food. I think next time, we're going to have to split a plate."

"I learned from your mother."

"Ha! I knew it," Greg said.

Isobel rolled her eyes. She thought from his tone that he was joking, but she said, "Ben, can you please tell him you're not pining away with unrequited love?"

"Do I look like I'm pining away?" He spread his hands questioningly. "I followed Isobel around in high school because I knew I wanted to be a chef and I wanted to steal her mother's recipes." He put on an excessively sad face. "Alas, it didn't work."

"For which you should be glad," Isobel said. "If your food were exactly like Momma's, there would be no reason for me to come back."

"I can live with that," he said. "Ken will be sad to have missed you, but if you come by on Friday, you can probably say hello. Besides," he added, "on Fridays, we do candlelight dinners on the patio and in the garden. Very romantic."

"Friday's going to be tough," Isobel said, "what with Summerfest."

"I'm counting on it," Ben said. "I could use a quiet night."

Isobel laughed. "We'll let you know."

He nodded. "If you have time before you leave today, you should walk around and visit the gardens. There's a waterwheel hidden in the center that most people never find. Very secluded."

"Next time," Greg said. "We actually have an appointment with a real estate agent in half an hour, so we should get moving."

"A Realtor?" Ben raised his eyebrows. "I'll have Chrissy bring you the check."

Before Isobel could protest that it wasn't like that, Ben had left. She slumped dramatically to the table. "It's a good thing I already told Momma why I'm helping you. The gossips are going to have us moving in together before the day is out."

"That would be problematic," Greg said seriously. "Your place is too small, and since mine's a sublet, there's nowhere for your stuff."

"That's not what I meant." She glared at him without moving.

He grinned back, unrepentant. "It's what you said."

"Here's your check. Did you want to-go boxes for your leftovers?"

"Why not?" Isobel said. "We can drop them in my refrigerator before we...head off for the day."

Greg glanced at the check, then handed it back to Chrissy along with a credit card. After she left, he said, "I'm going to have to over-tip. They didn't charge us for your food."

"I'll talk to Ben about that. Or maybe to Ken, when I see him. He always had the better head for business. You wouldn't believe how much money he made on his first lemonade stand."

"So what's the story about Ben and Ken? Best friends? Brothers? Another reason I don't have to be jealous?"

"They're cousins—second cousins, maybe? Or third? Kissing cousins, anyway, Momma would say. And best friends, of course. Born two days apart, and pretty much inseparable since. I don't know why it took them so long to open a restaurant; they've been talking about it for years."

"Money, most likely. Restaurants aren't cheap, and it looks like they did some heavy remodeling before they opened. The lease on this place must be—"

"That's one thing they don't have to worry about. It was in the family. I'm pretty sure one of them inherited it. Momma would know the details. Or Aunt Rosa. But if you ask, you're going to wind up hearing their entire family history, including who owned the place first, and how so-and-so's wife was no better than she ought to be, and on and on."

"No better than she ought to be. I like the sound of that."

She was saved from replying by Chrissy's return with the credit card receipt to sign and the to-go boxes. "Thanks. Please come again."

"We will," Greg said, smiling warmly at her. "The food is excellent, and the service is even better."

She blushed and left, taking the signed receipt with her.

"You flirt," Isobel said. "Can't take you anywhere."

"Hmm. Maybe we should go somewhere private, then."

Isobel stood up. "Right. I thought we were all going together in the real estate agent's car."

Greg slid his arm around her shoulders. "I guess I'll just have to plot for later, then."

CHAPTER FIFTEEN

Saturday, June 19, morning

The first house was a simple white ranch house. Isobel frowned as she got out of the car. "You know my Aunt Rosa lives just a block over?"

"Oh, good, you have family in the area," the agent gushed. Isobel stared at her, wondering how she'd managed to miss the entire conversation about why Isobel was coming along. Probably too busy counting her commission to pay attention.

Greg looked at Isobel. "Should we look anyway? We're here, and maybe your mother won't think I'm picking sides."

Isobel laughed hollowly and followed him into the house. "She'll be convinced Aunt Rosa knows more than she does—and Aunt Rosa will tell her that's true, even if it isn't."

Even with the curtains open and all of the lights on, the interior felt dark and dated. Walnut-colored paneling covered three of the living room walls, and the fourth was taken up by a wallpaper mural depicting a hunter about to shoot a deer. The carpet was orange shag with occasional darker spots.

"Maybe we should skip it, then," Greg said.

"No, we can look. It *is* a good neighborhood."

"The house has only had one set of owners," the agent said. "They recently moved into a retirement community, which is why this jewel is on the market."

Retirement community? Either they had moved out of River Corners entirely, or their nearest relatives had checked them into the Sunny Skies Nursing Home. The house sale was probably going to help support their stay there.

A doorway to the left gave onto a galley kitchen. It was larger than Isobel's kitchenette, but far smaller than Momma's kitchen. The chrome dishwasher looked as if it had been replaced within the past half dozen years, but the countertops were aged Formica.

The agent blathered on about work triangles, how well the room was set up, and how convenient it was to the garage for bringing in groceries. Greg bumped against her as he moved around, opening cupboards and peering inside. Everything appeared clean and in decent condition, although the glue traps under the sink did give Isobel pause.

Isobel wandered down the hallway toward the bedrooms. A door off to her right was open, and she looked in—the bathroom, also using the same orange shag carpeting, despite the avocado green tub, toilet, and sink. She wasn't sure which was worse—the color combination, or putting carpet in the bathroom in the first place.

The orange carpet had been swapped out for gold in the two bedrooms. Neither of the rooms showed any signs of being remarkable, except for some brown stains in the corner of one room that Isobel didn't want to think about too much.

Back in the living room, Greg swept his gaze around one more time, then shook his head. "It's got good bones, maybe, but it would take time or money—or both—to update it. What else do you have?"

The agent's face fell, but she rallied. "The next one's on the other side of town, in a newer subdivision. You wouldn't have to update it, but the neighborhood doesn't have a lot of character yet."

"How big is it?"

"A couple thousand feet—large enough for a young couple just settling down."

Greg nodded without saying anything and led the way out the door. While the agent fiddled with the lockbox for the key, Isobel muttered, "I'm beginning to think me coming with you was a mistake. Everyone's going to assume the same thing Momma did."

He took a step back and looked at her with eyebrows raised. "You told your mother you were house hunting with me?"

"If I didn't, and she found out—and she *would* find out—it would be so much worse."

"There is that." He held the car door open for her and dropped a kiss on the top of her head as she got in.

The next house was every bit as bland from the outside as the agent had promised—fake rock siding on the bottom half, false shutters outside the windows, and the same layout as every third house on the block, and the same "For Sale" sign as every other house. Young maple trees sat to either side of the driveway, and junipers lined the walkway to the front door. The large semicircular window over the front door hinted at spaciousness with lots of natural light, which at least was something.

That appeared to be most of what the house had going for it—large glass doors off the kitchen and dining area let in even more light. The cheerful yellow paint practically glowed. "At night, I'd probably look jaundiced," Isobel said.

Greg chuckled, and the agent shot her a dirty look. Isobel decided to let the agent showcase the house's finer points for Greg while she poked around at the nooks and crannies. To her surprise, the door immediately to the right of the front door led not to a bathroom but to a home office with built-in shelving and cabinets, a window seat, and a fireplace for the colder months. It was all bland faux wood—probably the same as the kitchen—but it looked cozy. She could imagine spending lots of time in here, marking up manuscripts or reading books. She blushed; now she was the one being presumptuous.

Greg's voice floated down the hall from the bedrooms, so Isobel poked her head into the kitchen. Yes, the exact same cabinets as in the office. Plenty of room to move around in, though, which was good, and even a big central island. Very nice.

She passed through the kitchen to a door set on the far right. Opening it, she saw the washer and dryer hook-ups on the left, a small mud area—shelves for boots and hangers for coats and wraps, plus a container for umbrellas (as evidenced by the black one someone had left behind during a previous showing—not recently, as it hadn't rained for a week) and a chest with a liftable lid (nothing had been left in there)—on the right. Straight ahead was the door to the garage. Garages struck Isobel as all very much the same (even more so in a subdivision like this one), but she went inside anyway.

It was a two-car garage, lined with the ubiquitous faux wood cabinetry of the house. One thing she had to say about the builders; they made certain that these houses had lots of storage space. She opened a couple of drawers, then moved over to peek into a couple of cabinets. Some sawdust sat on the shelving inside the lower cabinets. The next cabinet, a full-height one probably designed to hold rakes and shovels, didn't open readily when she tugged at it.

Frowning, she checked to see if there was a lock on the cabinet. She didn't see one. If Greg wanted to put an offer in on this house, he'd need to have the cabinets fixed. She kicked at the door, then tugged on it again. This time, the door opened.

A body slumped inside, face turned away from her. She shrieked in surprise.

Later she would tell herself that of course there was a body. Why wouldn't there be? She really ought to stop opening up random doors. Goodness only knew who she was going to find next time.

Now, however, she shrieked, slammed the door closed, turned, and ran back into the house.

Greg came to meet her, but the agent stood in the doorway of one of the bedrooms, laughing. "Did you find the surprise? Mary, the agent who's selling this house, thought the stuffed bear would be cute."

Isobel ignored the agent. "It's...it's..."

"Breathe." He caught her hands. "Are you okay? Do you need a glass of water?"

She shook her head. "No. No."

"Calm down. Tell me what's going on."

"It's...I have to call Michael. Again."

His eyebrows twitched upward. "Again? Not for the same reason?" His voice said that he didn't have much hope.

"Yes. I swear, he's going to think I did it on purpose."

"Can you show me?"

She noticed that he didn't bother denying Michael's attitude.

She nodded toward the kitchen. "This way."

The agent followed them, going on about how it had just been a practical joke, there was no reason to be upset or make a big deal about this. Isobel did her best to tune the agent out.

"Over here." Isobel motioned to the cupboard, but waved Greg away when he would have opened it. "My fingerprints are already on it. Let's keep it simple."

This time, the door opened more readily. Knowing what was inside, she didn't jump and shriek this time, but she did grin when the agent did both.

Then she sobered, taking in everything that she hadn't had time for before—dried blood on the framing, which had most likely contributed to the door being stuck closed; the bloody putter next to the body; the matted hair that looked familiar—

"It's the mayor!" the agent gasped.

The body snapped into focus, and Isobel recognized Richard Holstein. She knew better than to disturb a crime scene; Michael was already going to be upset. Still, she reached forward to turn his head and see his face better.

He moaned.

"He's still alive!" She touched his throat but couldn't find his pulse. "Not doing well, though." Isobel turned to see the agent with her cellphone out. "What are you doing?"

"Calling an ambulance! What do you think?" The agent glared at her. "I can't believe you didn't do it already."

"If I'd thought it would help…" she trailed off. She wasn't going to waste time defending herself to the agent. Instead, she pulled out her own cellphone and took a quick couple of pictures, then sent them to Michael.

The phone buzzed in her hand seconds later. "What did you do this time?"

"He's not dead, if it's any consolation."

Silence from the other end of the phone. "I just heard the dispatch for the ambulance. Stay put until I get there. And tell Stone—no, I'll tell him when I get there myself."

She hung up and frowned at her phone, then slid it back into her messenger bag. "He's on his way. And he's not happy with me."

"I noticed you didn't say that you didn't do it this time," Greg teased.

She shrugged off his attempt at humor. "I wonder if that's the same putter that was used on Father Paul."

"They can check that, I'm sure. It is from the minigolf course—I can see the name."

Now that he'd mentioned it, Isobel saw the glint of light off the gold engraving along the handle. It could be the same one—or it could be someone who didn't like Richard and wanted to make it look the same. Madge would know for certain. Isobel wondered if getting Father Paul's blood, even dried, mixed with his own created a health hazard for Richard. Realizing that she was about to break out in hysterical giggling, Isobel turned away.

The agent looked from one to the other of them as though they were crazy. "Who did you call? You couldn't even do something useful and call for an ambulance! And sending pictures? What, you have a family member who's a reporter? That's just sick. Well, they're not going to get in here. I'll make sure of that."

Isobel threw her shoulders back; she didn't have to take that kind of attitude.

Then Greg touched her on the arm and shook his head gently. "Fighting isn't going to solve anything."

"Fine. But I'm going to want an apology from her when she finds out she's wrong."

"Ha!" The agent glared at Greg. "You should find a new real estate agent. I don't like problem clients."

Isobel stiffened. How dare the agent blame Greg, as if he had been the one who attacked Richard and put him here in the garage? And why here, anyway? Richard Holstein wasn't as out of place here as Father Paul had been at the minigolf course, certainly; everyone who lived here probably wore suits to work and golfed—real golf, not putt-putt golf—on Wednesdays and Saturdays every week. This wasn't where the Holsteins lived, though, and Isobel doubted he was shopping for a new home.

She studied Richard's body, doing her best to ignore the agent's comments and Greg's calm responses. She didn't dare move him; she might hurt him more. She couldn't decide whether he'd been attacked where he was or not; the cabinet walls didn't show big splatters of blood, but there wasn't any on the garage floor, either. There *was* a lot on the floor of the cabinet—head wounds bled a lot, didn't they? Maybe it hadn't splattered at all, but just kept bleeding.

An approaching siren cut through the conversation, and Greg broke off what he was saying to go push the automatic door opener. After a second, he pushed the button for the door opener for the other side of the garage as well, letting more light spill in.

The agent went outside to flag down the ambulance. Greg came to stand next to Isobel, and she leaned on him. "I don't know which is worse, sometimes—the people who don't know who my family is, or the ones who do."

He squeezed her shoulders. "Must be quite a shock for you, running into two people in one week who don't know your cousin's the police chief."

She chuckled. "I remember how pleased you were when you learned the police chief is my cousin."

"Mmm. Much better than the alternative." He squeezed her again, then let her go. "On the other hand, it does mean I see a lot more of law enforcement than I'd ever expected."

A car door slammed in the driveway, and Isobel gave Greg a wry grin. "Brace yourself. You're about to see him again."

CHAPTER SIXTEEN

Saturday, June 19, still morning

"You couldn't have just called me?" Michael didn't bother with "hello."

"I wasn't sure you'd get here before the ambulance, and I wanted you to see what he looks like." Isobel nodded to Officer Gray, behind Michael. "I did move his head."

Michael grimaced. "Tell the paramedics. If he's got any spinal cord trauma, they'll need to know that." He nodded to Gray. "Get some pictures, quickly, then get out of the way."

Gray started snapping pictures, flash strobing.

"How'd you find him?"

Isobel shrugged. "I was poking around at the cabinets. That one wouldn't open, and then it did. Gave me quite a shock."

"You could hear her scream on the other end of the house," Greg put in.

"So she's quieted down as she got older, then."

Isobel glared at her cousin. "I wasn't expecting to find a body in the garage."

"You surprise me. I would think by now you expect to find a body every time you walk into a new place."

She crossed her arms and peered up at him, annoyed at him echoing her own thoughts. "It's not my fault."

"Of course not." He stepped forward and patted her on the head, then laughed as she snapped her teeth at him. "Trouble follows you around, and sometimes it gets there first."

The paramedics wheeled in a gurney, with the agent following them, talking even faster than when she was describing a house. "And they didn't even have the sense to call, and she could have hurt him more, and…"

Michael cut across her chatter. "Where are you going to take him?"

"The clinic. They can make sure he's stable, do an X-ray, check to see if there is any spinal damage, then see about transferring him up to Majors." Majors was the closest large hospital. If you needed anything more specialized than a cast for a broken leg, you went to Majors. "Do you know whether he has insurance?"

Michael nodded. "The city provides it. I'll have his wife meet you at the hospital, in case his insurance card's not in his wallet."

The paramedic nodded, then turned to the cabinet. Getting Richard out of his slumped sitting position and onto the gurney without twisting his spine was going to be difficult. Isobel watched with fascination as they slid a board behind him, bracing his head so it didn't flop, then fastened straps across him to hold him in place. Next, one grabbed his legs and pulled, while the other held the top of the board—an impressive feat given the strange angle he was at. Finally, they lifted him onto the gurney, board still in place.

Officer Gray took pictures of the entire procedure. Everything had to be documented.

Isobel turned back to ask Michael a question but saw he was on his phone. Talking to Sue, no doubt. Isobel felt a twinge of sympathy for Sue. At least Richard wasn't dead.

Greg moved closer to her and took her hand in his. Isobel gave him a grateful smile.

Michael closed his phone, then swept his gaze around the garage. "Gray, get a couple patrolmen to sweep the neighborhood, see if anyone saw anything." He waited while Gray left the garage through the open door, then pulled a notepad and pencil from his pocket and pointed at the agent. "This house is for sale, right? How hard is it to get into it? Is there any way to track who's been in and out?"

The agent shook her head. "Anyone with the code could get in, any time. And one of the bedroom windows was open—"

Michael groaned and made a note on his pad, but waved for her to continue.

"That's about it, really. It's not hard to get in, if you know how, and with the window open, anyone could've come in."

"Tell me about the house. Who has it listed? Does it have a security system? Motion sensitive lights? Anything to make the job of the police easier?"

Isobel hid a small smile. Although Michael didn't have anything on his house besides good locks, he'd badgered his mother into getting motion sensitive lights recently, and he'd been at Momma to do the same. He hadn't been after Isobel because Kimberley's house already had lights and security—although the security system didn't include the cottage Isobel lived in.

The agent shrugged. "It's a new house. The developer's selling it. A security system is an add-on, makes the houses more expensive, so only a few of them have it built in."

"Why'd you pick this house to show this morning?" Michael wasn't finished with her.

"It's available. Mister Stone wasn't very specific about what he was looking for, so I'm showing him a range of houses. That way, we can nail it down. This one's newer and would require less upkeep than some of the older ones." She motioned at the cabinetry as evidence of the newness of the construction, wincing as she looked at the open cabinet with Richard's blood still in it, reddish brown on the bottom, as well as against the wall where his head had been leaning.

"Was showing," Greg put in, drawing everyone's attention back to the center of the garage.

"Was showing," she reluctantly agreed. "I...was intemperate in my language when his girlfriend found the victim, and I blamed him."

Michael's lips twitched when the agent referred to Isobel only as Greg's girlfriend, but he didn't comment on that. Instead, he asked, "Did you recognize the victim?"

"Of course. Everyone knows Mayor Holstein." The agent looked at Michael as though he had brain damage.

"What dealings have you had with the mayor before?"

"I don't like the tone of your questions!"

Isobel buried her face against Greg's chest to hide her grin. Good for Michael for making the agent squirm! The agent's attitude had really gotten under Isobel's skin, and she was glad to see the agent get a taste of her own medicine.

"What?" Michael's tone was mild. "Do you have a problem telling me how well you know him?"

"You're implying that I had something to do with this!"

"No, I'm doing my job, which includes talking to witnesses and learning their background with the victim. If you prefer, you can come with me down to the station and we can do this formally."

"I don't see you asking Miss-High-and-Mighty there, and she's the one who found the body!"

Isobel risked a glance at her cousin. He was looking at her with his best butter-wouldn't-melt-in-his-mouth expression. "Isobel, are you still nursing a grudge because Richard beat you in the pie-eating contest when you were in fifth grade?"

"He cheated! He was five years older than me, and he put dirt on my pie!"

"Very well, then. I can see this case is solved. I'll just have to take you in."

"All right, but I'll have Aunt Rosa bake me a cake with a file in it so I can break out."

"You two aren't taking this seriously!" the agent sputtered.

"On the contrary," Michael said, "I'm taking this very seriously. Someone attacked the mayor and tried to kill him. You are among the people I know had access to this place. We'll compile a list and talk to everyone else, but right now, you're here, so you're being questioned. If you were the attacker, it would make perfect sense to make sure that someone else was here to discover the body."

"Unless the attacker didn't want the body found. Why else use an abandoned house?"

"Fewer witnesses than the middle of the street," Greg said. When everyone looked at him, he said, "What? It's true. The neighborhood's half empty, so the people moving in probably pay attention to new neighbors and goings-on outside. I'll bet there are half a dozen people on their lawns or peering out their windows right now, wondering what the ambulance was doing here and why there's still a police car parked out front."

Isobel nodded. "And with so many houses for sale still, the attacker may have figured the odds were on Richard not being discovered just yet."

"Plenty of time to establish an alibi," Greg added.

Michael glowered at the pair of them. "Are you two done doing my job?"

"For now." Greg held Isobel for a second, then let her go. "Are we done here?"

The Miniature Golf Course Murders

"You have something more pressing to do?"

"I suppose not," Greg said easily. "The plan was to spend the day house-hunting, but that looks like a bust."

"You could check out some open houses. Later, you two can tell me all about the wonderful houses you found."

Heat rushed to Isobel's face. She'd known this was coming, but Michael had still managed to catch her off guard. She opened her mouth to tell him they weren't looking together, but the agent cut in.

"Open houses are on Sunday, not Saturday."

"Well, then, the pair of you can go tomorrow after church."

"Michael…"

"Just go, Isobel. I've got work to do."

Isobel glanced over at the agent, who said, "I suppose I can give you a ride back to your car."

"Don't sound so thrilled."

"Why should I? Because of you, I've lost a client, and the police think I'm a suspect in attempted murder."

Isobel glanced at Michael. "Any chance you could give us a ride instead? We can just sit quietly and not touch anything until you're ready to go."

"Promise? No more bodies?"

"Cross my heart." Isobel matched the words with the motion. "If there are any more bodies around, I won't find them." She thought for a minute, then added, "Today."

Michael shook his head. "I guess that's the best I'm going to get from you." A smile lit his face. "The only place my car has room is in the back. You don't mind riding in the back of a police car, do you? Even if it smells like rotten eggs?"

She had said that, hadn't she? "As long as you let us out at the other end."

"Hmm. If I don't, it would keep you out of trouble." He stroked his chin thoughtfully.

"Is that a challenge?"

"No," Michael and Greg said simultaneously.

Isobel looked back and forth between them. "Sometimes, you're no fun!"

CHAPTER SEVENTEEN

Saturday, June 19, evening

Greg didn't stick around when he dropped her at her mother's house. He walked Isobel as far as the door, but said, "She's made it clear that these lessons are just for you."

"You just don't want to get a lecture about finding another body."

He didn't deny it. "Remind her that this one wasn't dead."

"You know she's still going to go on about the risks I'm taking."

He dropped a kiss on her forehead. "She loves you; she worries about you. Now go—make something incredible."

"I'll settle for edible." She pushed open the door—despite Momma's worries about Isobel, she never would lock her door in the middle of the day—and stepped inside. The aroma of lemon cookies greeted her, and she smiled fondly. "Who knows? Maybe she'll let me have a cookie for my trouble."

"I heard that!" Momma said from a chair in the living room. "You have to wait for my cookies just like the rest of the town."

Isobel smiled at Greg and closed the door. "You could teach me to make them."

Momma laughed without getting up. "I will, but not today. I thought today we'd do the easy Thanksgiving side dishes so you have practice with them—cranberry sauce and mashed sweet potatoes."

"Cranberries? At this time of year?" Isobel had already made mashed potatoes a few times under Momma's watchful eye. Cranberry sauce was new, though.

"I put them away in the freezer at Christmastime. I knew we'd need them." Momma stood. "You'll like this lesson; all you have to do is boil water. I know you can do that." She cocked her head at Isobel. "What's wrong? You're pale. You're not getting sick or anything, are you?"

Isobel shook her head. "I found—"

"Not another one?" Momma's tone was sharp.

"Richard Holstein." At Momma's gasp, Isobel added, "He's still alive, but he was unconscious. Someone hit him over the head with a putter. More than once, I think."

"Does his wife know?" Trust Momma not to use Sue's name if she didn't have to.

"Michael called her already. She was going to meet the ambulance at the hospital."

"I see." Momma headed toward the kitchen, calling over her shoulder, "This changes the plans, of course. We'll have to cook for her; she'll be simply too distraught to do anything."

"Momma, you're evil."

Momma's chuckle told Isobel that Momma knew exactly what she meant. Sue resented the way Momma and Aunt Rosa took charge of so much in the community—and Kimberley picked up the slack. Although Sue had been in town for at least a decade, she was still an outsider, an interloper who wanted to be the social queen and never would be. Taking her food was charity, work that Momma would do for anyone in the church, but it would also underline that Sue would never have the standing that Momma did.

"Tell me all about it before my sister calls."

"Yes, Momma." Isobel followed her mother into the kitchen and crossed to take a mug from the cupboard. "We were at this house in the new subdivision—"

Momma added water to her copper kettle and put it on the front burner to heat. "You may as well start at the beginning. When she calls, I need to know things she doesn't."

Of course. Michael would tell Aunt Rosa everything he knew, so the only way Momma could count herself morally superior was if she knew things Aunt Rosa didn't. Dutifully, Isobel began again.

"Greg picked me up this morning and took me to breakfast at the Farmhouse—he laughed when I told him I could make cinnamon rolls for breakfast!—and Ben made the most excellent waffle for me, covered with potatoes and greens and eggs. He still says he'd like to steal some of your recipes, though."

"That goes without saying." Momma handed Isobel a tea bag.

Isobel leaned her hip against the counter, taking care to keep her back straight.

"Yes, Momma. After breakfast, we dropped the leftovers at my place, then went over to meet the real estate agent at her office. I don't know her at all; she must be new here. The first house she took us to was on Elm, about a block from Aunt Rosa's."

"That'll be the Winters' place. They just moved into the River Village—in separate apartments, I understand."

Trust Momma to know all the details.

"The house was okay, but Greg thought it would take too much time and money to update it. It looks like it hasn't changed since the early seventies."

The kettle whistled, and Momma turned off the heat.

"That would be when they got the inheritance from her mother, so they had money to redecorate. Probably didn't want to spend money on it again, after that had cost so much." Momma poured the boiling water into Isobel's mug and one she'd fetched for herself. "It wouldn't be a bad place to live."

"After that, we went to the new subdivision—you know, the one they put in where the apple farm used to be? Half the houses are still for sale, so I think they overestimated the market."

"Might mean he could get a good price on one, then. Better they get some money than none."

"Maybe. It did have a lot of storage space—cabinets everywhere. I didn't see what the closets are like in the bedrooms, but the garage—well, the garage had a cabinet big enough to hide a body. And I found it. The agent kept going on about some stuffed bear put somewhere as a practical joke, but I didn't see that, just Richard."

Momma didn't answer at first. Finally, she shook her head. "I don't understand some people. But now, we cook—and you will make cinnamon rolls, too. For Sue. You know where the flour is. Get the dough started before we start work on the casseroles."

Isobel sighed. She should never have mentioned the cinnamon rolls. Maybe working with the dough would help her feel better, though. It always seemed to work for Momma.

She pulled yeast and eggs from the refrigerator. "Aunt Rosa hasn't called you to talk about the mayor yet. Maybe you should call her, have her make something, too?"

"Oh, so you don't think I can manage without my sister? A fine thing!"

"That's not it, at all." How should she put it? Sue Holstein had tried to drive a wedge between the two sisters more than once. What better way to present a united front? No, although it was true, it was too direct. "I just know that Aunt Rosa has every bit as much reason to care about Sue as you do."

"Hmph."

Isobel didn't need to look to know that Momma had crossed her arms in front of her. Because Isobel was right, of course, but Momma didn't want to say so.

"You get that dough together."

Isobel did, scalding milk (and hoping that she hadn't burned it on the bottom of the pan this time), adding butter to the milk to melt, and setting it aside to cool while she measured flour, sugar, salt, and yeast, then whisked them together. She poured some of the milk into the flour mixture, then cracked in the eggs. After blending those, she added the rest of the milk, turned the resulting dough out onto the counter, and began kneading.

Meanwhile, she listened to her momma's side of the phone conversation.

"Hello, Rosa. No, it's Maria Elena, of course. You're too busy to talk to me? Forgive me, it must be rough to have such a *busy* social calendar. Cooking? Oh, I *see*. And much too busy to call your own sister. Hmph." She hung up the phone with rather more force than necessary, and Isobel winced.

"That woman!" Momma didn't even give Isobel the chance to ask what was wrong. "Told me I needn't bother with any cooking for Sue Holstein, as *she* already called the Ladies' Altar Society phone chain. None of whom called me, of course, including my own sister."

Isobel paused with her hands still in the dough. "What are we going to do then?"

"What do you think? We're going to cook. No one, not even my sister, is going to tell me I'm not necessary. Is that dough ready to rise now? Put it on the warming shelf while we put the first casserole together." She kept talking with her head in the refrigerator, while pulling out various ingredients. "Might as well use the cranberries in the casserole, don't want to refreeze them. Maybe we can do a Thanksgiving casserole…yes, I have turkey in the freezer. Your lucky day, Isobel—you get to learn to make stuffing, too. Start by tearing up the bread. And when you're done, peel the potatoes and put them on to boil."

After covering the dough with a kitchen towel and setting it aside to rise, Isobel washed her hands and started cleaning off the counter where she'd been working on the dough. "We're going to put mashed potatoes into the casserole?"

Some people did, she was sure, but if they were doing that, then why the stuffing?

"Don't be silly. The mashed potatoes are for gnocchi. No one else will be making those!"

"Probably not," Isobel agreed. "Are you sure she knows what to do with them? You don't want them to go to waste."

Momma frowned, then nodded decisively. "I'll put a card on top with the cooking instructions. Even if she is upset, she should be able to follow instructions."

Should be able to didn't mean Sue would, but Isobel didn't say so. Instead, she reached for the bread and began tearing it up into a large bowl. "You're going to need more eggs, Momma."

"Only use three. We're just making enough stuffing for the casserole, not to feed the family." She smiled. "Then I'll have enough through Monday, when I go to the store again." She pointed at Isobel's tea. "Are you going to drink that before it gets cold?"

Sheepishly, Isobel removed her tea bag and took a sip. It wasn't as bad as she'd feared—still warm, though not hot. She drank some more.

"So the casserole is going to be turkey, cranberries, and stuffing? Won't that be a little dry?"

"Don't be silly. We'll have gravy in there as well." Momma opened the freezer and started shuffling containers around. "I was sure I had some saved in here…your cousin must have eaten it all. You'll just have to make more."

Isobel panicked. "Again? I didn't even remember to strain it last night. And it only turned out so tasty because I was starting with the juice from the roast!"

Momma pulled two plastic bags out of the freezer and started running them under the tap. "You'll be fine. Finish the bread first. Then we'll brown the turkey in butter, add a little flour, deglaze the pan with broth, and instant gravy."

A packet from the store that she mixed with water seemed more like instant gravy to Isobel, but she didn't say so. Instead, she kept tearing at the bread, shredding the cubes further and further into tiny pieces.

"Enough! We're not trying to bread the turkey." She handed one of the plastic bags to Isobel. "This is for the gravy. I'll use the other one for the stuffing. Pay attention because we won't do this again until October or so. Stuffing really is a cool weather dish."

Isobel grabbed a notecard and pencil from next to the phone, ignoring her momma's put-upon sigh. If Isobel wasn't going to be doing this again for four months, she was going to need notes to work from. First, she jotted down the torn loaf of bread, adding "(not crumbs)." Then she looked expectantly at her mother. It was too much to ask that her mother use actual measurements, but Isobel did her best to guess. She was sure she'd hear about her shortcomings in October anyway, even with the notes.

Once the stuffing and the gravy were prepared, assembling the dish was relatively quick, layering the ingredients just so. "Sprinkle some sugar on the cranberries. And just a splash of brandy."

"I don't think Sue drinks."

Momma sniffed. "Just add it." After a moment, she added, "She does sometimes. I've seen her. At the pageant, when she thought no one was looking, she slipped something into her cider."

Isobel raised her eyebrows. Momma had seen that and not said anything for six months? That was impressive.

Finally, Momma pronounced the casserole ready to go into the oven. "Let's see my sister top that!"

Isobel just smiled as she took the sweet dough down to roll out for the cinnamon rolls. Spending time with her Momma cooking was certainly instructive, and not just about recipes.

CHAPTER EIGHTEEN

Sunday, June 20

The next morning, Isobel stopped to pick up Momma before Mass.

"Now remember, we have to take this food by the Holsteins'," Momma said when she opened the door.

"I thought we'd do that after church."

"And leave it in the car? In the heat? I'm sure you know better than that!" Momma brushed past Isobel, carrying the tray of cinnamon rolls. Sighing, Isobel stacked the two casserole dishes and followed her momma out to the car.

The cars in front of the Holstein house showed that they weren't the only ones with this idea. Momma pointed at the driveway, and, sighing, Isobel pulled in behind the two cars that were already there, even though it left the rear end of her car poking into the street.

Mary Beth Scott answered the door when they rang. Surprise flickered across her face. "Why, Maria Elena, you're such good people. I remember when you dropped by with a casserole for me last winter."

"So why are you so shocked to see me here?" Momma asked bluntly. "And why didn't you call me when you did the phone chain?"

"When Rosa called me, she told me you were busy, so I should skip you." Mary Beth stepped back to let them inside.

Isobel noted the heavy wooden furniture, the spotless white carpet, and the glass coffee table. Either Sue had too much time on her hands or she hired a cleaning service, probably the latter. Isobel was sure it looked good when Richard had Council members over for dinner, though—or campaign donors.

The room looked as carefully crafted to project an image as Momma's living room.

"If you'll just follow me to the kitchen, we can put those away. I see you even included reheating instructions. So thoughtful of you!"

"I try."

Mary Beth frowned over her shoulder. "I am not getting in the middle of a fight between you and your sister. I learned my lesson years ago."

Momma nodded and didn't press it. Isobel wanted to know what had happened between the three women, but she knew better than to ask. Sometimes, she still felt like she was in grade school.

If Isobel had expected the façade from the living room to fall away, as it did in Momma's house, she was shocked when she entered the kitchen. It was a showpiece from an architecture magazine, with white marble countertops, travertine backsplashes, and appliances artfully hidden behind maple cabinetry fronts. The only thing that appeared to get any use was the half-full coffeemaker set off to one side of the stove. She couldn't imagine Sue cooking in here.

Mary Beth opened up a full-length cabinet that exposed the refrigerator. Inside lay various covered casseroles, a half-dozen diet shakes, and some Chinese takeout boxes. No milk, no juice, no eggs—even Isobel kept those on hand! For a moment, she felt elated that she was a better cook than Sue, then immediately felt guilty for the thought.

"Those will fit right here on this shelf. I know Sue will appreciate them."

"*More* food?" Sue's voice came from off to one side; she had entered the kitchen from a different direction. "As if charity's not bad enough! How much do they think one person can eat?"

Momma's lips grew pinched, and Isobel knew she was holding back her first, caustic, reply. When she did speak, her tone was calm and measured. "When Richard gets out of the hospital, he's going to need food to get his strength back. We can put these in the freezer, if you prefer."

Sue heaved a sigh. She looked paler than usual, with her makeup not in place, and she had circles under her eyes. She reminded Isobel of Kimberley just after John had been killed. "Oh, no, I couldn't put you out. I'm sure Mary Beth will arrange everything. Why not? She simply moved in and took charge this morning; I'm sure the food storage is just one thing she's keeping track of."

"If you'd rather I leave—" Mary Beth began.

"What, so I'd have to answer the door to everyone who wants to traipse by? Thank you, no. I'll just go back and lie down and let you ladies get on with your charmed and spoiled lives where nothing ever goes wrong."

The three women stared after her retreating back wordlessly. Isobel knew she'd mostly had a good life, if you ignored her father's abandonment, but it had really been her mother he'd abandoned. And Mary Beth? She and her husband had been in danger of losing their livelihood this past winter with the murders on their farm. She opened her mouth to speak, then shut it again. Words didn't cover this, at least not ones she would use in front of Momma.

"Let's put your dishes in the freezer, then, shall we?" Mary Beth said after a moment. "I know Richard won't want to miss the chance to have some of your cooking. I'll rearrange the rest later." She glanced at her wristwatch. "You two had better get moving if you're going to make it to church. If you see Annie while you're there, have her stop by before she goes home, would you please?"

Parking at the church took even longer than usual. Isobel finally gave up and dropped Momma off near the front doors before driving around to the next block to park in front of a random house. Father Paul had been quite popular with the congregation, and she imagined that even the curmudgeons who hadn't liked him didn't want to miss the opportunity to hear Bishop Daniels.

She made it inside before the entrance antiphon, but not by much. Without taking her usual glance around at the warm wooden interior with its stained glass that gradually morphed from Matisse curves to Frank Lloyd Wright geometrics, Isobel headed down the gold carpet runner to their usual seating on the left side of the middle aisle, nodding to Drew Scott and other parishioners she knew along the way. She was still squeezing past others in the pew to sit next to Momma when the organist played the first notes and the congregation rose. Slipping her messenger bag under the well-worn wooden pew, she turned to watch the procession.

Annie, garbed as an altar server with an alb over her street clothes and her hair pulled neatly back with a matching white headband, carried the processional cross. She was getting a little old to be an altar server, but as long as she was still in high school, there was no reason for her not to be. Isobel wondered whether it counted toward her community service hours for graduation.

Behind Annie came a pair of much younger altar boys, one swinging a censer filled with incense (Isobel rubbed her nose reflexively), the other with his hands clasped together. Next came a lector, bearing high the Bible that would be used during the Mass, then Father Terrence and one of the deacons (whose names Isobel could never keep straight), with Bishop Daniels bringing up the rear.

It being Sunday, this wasn't a funeral Mass; the readings were the same as they would be in every other Catholic church that day. No one was surprised, however, when the bishop stood up to give the homily and started off by saying that, important as the day's readings were, he would not be touching on them while he spoke of Father Paul. Rustling quickly died down as people settled in to listen.

"Today, I want to talk to you about wickedness and sin. It's not a popular thing, at least in our Church, to talk about people's inherent sinfulness. We have Reconciliation rather than Penance for wrongdoings, and many don't even worry about this Sacrament at all, taking the Eucharist each week as their due for showing up. We don't examine our own consciences, and if we think about wickedness, it's in a finger-pointing 'Look what they did' sort of way.

"However—we are *all* guilty. We are all sinners, and the evil that allowed someone to strike down Paul and attempt to do the same to your mayor—that evil exists in all of us."

Isobel had expected a homily that talked about how loved Father Paul was. Talking about whoever had attacked made sense, she supposed, but didn't it put the emphasis on the wrong thing, taking it away from all the good that Father Paul had done? Judging by the murmurs around her, she wasn't the only one surprised by the bishop's choice.

"The first murder was brother of brother—Cain slew Abel, the beloved of the Lord. All of us have that sin within us, the capability of killing another, the culpability for all that we have done. Here, in this community, someone else has slain a beloved of the Lord, one who vowed to serve him, one who was loved by all who knew him."

Two rows in front of Isobel, Sadie scowled. Maybe not quite all.

"As a community, you are all guilty. You may not have lifted your hand to strike the blow, but you have turned a blind eye to sin and wickedness, giving it a place to thrive so this evil could be done. Today, as you come forward to receive the Eucharist, the body and blood of Christ, remember all the blood that is upon your hands."

He turned to walk back to his seat, then turned back to face the congregation once again. "Pray for your souls, and for the life of Richard Holstein, who still may fall to this evil."

The entire congregation sat in stunned silence as the offertory hymn began and the gifts were brought forward to the altar to be blessed. It wasn't fire and brimstone, but it was a far cry from the calls to love their neighbor and feed the poor that the congregants usually heard.

Isobel pulled her messenger bag out from beneath the pew and rummaged around for her envelope for the collection. The check she'd written was larger than usual this week—only by five dollars, but larger. Was she trying to salve a guilty conscience?

She didn't think she was responsible for Father Paul being killed, no matter what Bishop Daniels had said. She hadn't killed him, and she hadn't encouraged anyone else in their ill feelings toward him. Her gaze slid forward to Sadie again. But could she have done more to prevent this? Or if she had found Father Paul sooner, not dallied on the course with Greg, might he have still been alive, as Richard had been?

Brushing these thoughts away, she dropped her envelope into the collection basket. *Someone* was guilty. Someone had killed Father Paul and tried to kill Richard Holstein. Isobel could do her part to bring that person's actions to light and excise that wickedness from the community. That might not have been the bishop's point, but it was what she could do.

CHAPTER NINETEEN

Sunday, June 20, after church

"Momma, you go on ahead without me. I just need to make a quick stop."

To Isobel's relief, her momma thought of the obvious. "Quick? I've seen the line for the restroom before. I'll try to save you a doughnut or two."

Isobel smiled her relief and headed down the hallway. She drank from the water fountain, using the opportunity to make sure her momma had gone ahead to the fellowship hall and the receptionist was busy answering questions. Then she strolled down the connecting corridor that led to the priest's offices. Father Paul's office had his name on the door, and to her relief, the door was open as if he had just stepped out for a minute.

Feeling a mix of grief and guilt, Isobel stepped inside. She'd never been in the priest's office, and she was surprised at how normal it looked—windows to her left bracketed by file cabinets; desk to her right with two chairs in front of it for visitors; and a nook in the back with a bookcase, a credenza, and a large wall calendar with dates filled in. The calendar didn't show daily appointments—weddings were noted, Summerfest was blocked off, and Sundays were marked with a rotation of names in the order the priests said Mass. He probably kept more immediate appointments in an electronic calendar, but his computer (an Apple, according to the logo front and center) wasn't on and she didn't think she would have time to boot it up.

Her curiosity made her look at the bookshelves—she couldn't pass a bookcase without looking to see what other people thought worth keeping. Mostly theology, unsurprisingly, although he did have one shelf filled with works by G. K. Chesterton, Dorothy L. Sayers, and Andrew Greeley. A mystery fan who got to star in his very own murder mystery.

What else?

The pictures behind his desk were unexceptional—a framed print of the Pope, a picture of Father Paul with a group of other priests—probably from seminary, and a shot of him with a woman who had to be his sister. The desk itself was obsessively tidy; he probably got along quite well with Kimberley. The only paper left out was a pad of Post-It notes next to the phone. The top sheet showed some impressions, and she tore it off and stuffed it into her pocket to look at later.

"Can I help you?"

Isobel started. Father Terrence glowered at her from the doorway. Behind him, she saw Drew Scott glance in as he walked past, but Drew didn't stop.

"I'm sorry." Her face heated, and she fumbled for an excuse to be in the office. "I was just—Father Paul was supposed to give the opening prayer for Summerfest—"

"Yes. And?"

"I was looking for his notes. Kimberley—Mrs. Ansel—asked for my help, so since I was here, I thought I'd just have a quick look." She hoped Kimberley would back her up on this. "I didn't want to disturb anyone. I'm sorry."

If anything, his frown deepened. "I wasn't aware a replacement for his duties had been chosen."

"Not yet, but you know Kimberley. Anything to make things run more smoothly, everything choreographed to the second, nothing left to chance…" Aware that she was babbling, Isobel stopped.

"I see." He stepped to one side and motioned for her to leave the office. "I'll see what I can find. Have her make an appointment to see me, and I'll give her what there is."

She nodded, eager to escape. Slipping into the hallway, she barely stopped herself from apologizing again.

Stragglers from church were still heading upstairs; she hadn't taken as long as she had feared. Isobel joined them. She hoped that the note she had found was something useful.

The crowd in the fellowship hall was even larger than usual after Mass; Father Paul had been well loved. Some of the older congregants pressed around the bishop, thanking him for his honesty and forthrightness. Isobel took advantage of the crowd to slip past without greeting him. Momma was sure to castigate her later for her rudeness, but Isobel couldn't bring herself to care.

Tables along the far wall had tray after tray of doughnuts, and coffee urns had been set up at the right end of the wall, next to the kitchen doors. Isobel reached between a couple of other parishioners to grab a powdered sugar doughnut and a paper napkin. Turning around, she found herself facing Michael, whose longer reach had allowed him to snag not one but two apple fritters and an old-fashioned.

"That was interesting," she said by way of greeting.

He shrugged. "He's not calling for my head, I can live with it."

She laughed, spraying powdered sugar. Quickly, she brought her napkin up to cover her face. Michael heaved a long-suffering sigh and brushed the powdered sugar off his shirt front.

"I take it the newspaper has been less than favorable?" She had the headlines, including Op-Ed, e-mailed to her every day, so she knew that it had been. This made a more sympathetic opening than telling him she'd read it, though.

"When isn't it?" Michael took a large bite of an apple fritter and chewed it thoughtfully. "It's a good spread today. Much better than last week."

Isobel nodded. "I'm impressed that Mary Beth found time to organize this, what with her taking care of Sue."

"And how do you know that?" Aunt Rosa asked, appearing next to her son.

"Hello, Ma," he said. "Old-fashioned?"

"You know I prefer maple bars," she chided. She peered at Isobel. "Just how do you know that Mary Beth is taking care of Sue Holstein? You're not in the Altar Society."

Isobel ignored her cousin's snort. "Momma and I stopped by on the way here."

"I *told* her she didn't need to cook anything."

"Would that stop you?"

"That is beside the point, young lady. Now there's going to be too much food. I had this carefully planned."

"A plan that conveniently left me out, I notice." Momma handed Isobel a paper cup with pale orange-brown liquid inside. "It's all they had for tea."

"Thank you, Momma," Isobel said, although she didn't think her momma heard her over Aunt Rosa's raised voice.

"I was trying to do you a favor! I know how you're trying to get ready for Summerfest, so I give my sister some extra time, and what does she do? She ignores me!"

"Give me time? You were trying to cut me out." Momma sniffed. "Though given how ungrateful *she* was, maybe I should have been baking cookies instead."

Aunt Rosa said, "It's how she is. You know she can't acknowledge that someone else did something nice."

"It was worse than that," Isobel said. "She said we lived 'charmed and spoiled lives.'"

Michael smothered a chuckle, and Aunt Rosa sniffed. "She should know from spoiled."

This time, both Isobel and Michael tried to contain their amusement. Sue was going through a rough time, but that didn't excuse the way she acted the rest of the time. Spoiled didn't even begin to cover it.

"Excuse me, could I get through?" one of Momma's neighbors asked. "I do want to get a doughnut before they're all gone this week."

Michael glanced around the room. "There's some open space over in the far corner, near the windows. How about we move that way?"

"We'll follow you," his mother said. "People get out of your way."

People would move quickly enough for Momma and Aunt Rosa, too, but no one pointed this out. If Aunt Rosa wanted to pretend she didn't know that, so be it.

The corner wasn't exactly empty—the room was much too crowded for that—but Drew Scott raised his coffee cup in a companionable greeting. "So, Isobel, you going to solve this one, too?"

She took refuge in her weak tea. He'd seen her in Father Paul's office, so he knew she was snooping. She just hoped he had the sense not to say so in front of her cousin.

Michael spoke up. "We've talked about this, Isobel. Remember? You're supposed to do your best to stay out of danger. Your knight in shining armor might not be around to rescue you next time."

"I didn't say—"

He cut her protest off. "You didn't say you weren't, either. And I know you were talking to the mayor, remember? Did you think that maybe that's why he was attacked? Because he talked to you and someone thought he might know something incriminating?"

"Wouldn't it make more sense for them to attack him before he talked to me, then?"

"Like someone who goes around hitting people over the head with minigolf putters is rational!" His voice had gotten louder, and conversations nearby faded as people listened in.

Isobel noticed the parishioners watching and bit her upper lip. "I don't think this is—"

"Of course you don't think. That's my point. Stick to your job and let me do mine!"

Annie pushed through the crowd and addressed Drew, ignoring the tension. "Hi, Grand-pop. Is it okay if I catch a ride home with Frank? I promised to help clean up."

He raised his eyebrows. "As long as you're home in time for supper, it's fine with me. Might want to check with your mom, though."

"Pfft. She's already vanished. God only knows what she's decided to go take pictures of this time. Or maybe she's back at work on her book. I know she certainly doesn't tell me."

He frowned a bit at her, and was about to say something when Isobel spoke up. "Actually, your grandmother asked if you could stop by the Holstein house before you head home. You might want to do that after you clean up here."

"And before I do anything else?" Annie grinned.

"You said it, I didn't."

Drew huffed, but Isobel noticed that the corners of his eyes were crinkled as if he were suppressing a smile. "Isobel, you shouldn't encourage her."

Isobel shrugged. "She takes after her mother and grandmother—takes on anything that she wants, and has the guts and the willingness to keep going until she gets it."

Aunt Rosa laughed. "True enough. You should have seen Mary Beth chase him."

"She did not!" But Drew's cheeks were pink, and he wouldn't meet anyone's eyes.

"See you at home, Grand-pop." Annie leaned in and kissed his cheek. "I promise I won't stay out too late."

Michael wasn't about to let a little interruption halt his lecture. As soon as Annie walked away, he lowered his eyebrows and stepped closer to Isobel, forcing her to crane her neck to look up at him. "I don't want to hear any more about you solving a murder. You are not Miss Marple or Nancy Drew, and I don't think even your thick skull could resist being bashed in."

Nettled, she poked his chest. "If you don't want me to ask questions, then maybe you should solve the crimes."

"Thanks for the support." He turned and stalked off.

Both Aunt Rosa and Momma were staring at her, but neither one of them said anything. Isobel swallowed. She hadn't thought that was possible.

Drew cleared his throat. "Sorry, Isobel. Didn't mean to cause a family squabble."

Momma said, "Think nothing of it. We were just leaving."

Isobel followed Momma out of the room. The crowd around the bishop had thinned, but it didn't look as though he'd managed to get either a doughnut or coffee for himself yet. Jim Butler was talking to him now.

"What you said in there—I do feel it. I feel guilty. My car lot is right next door to where Father Paul died. You should check us out, best deals in the state. But I was right there, and he died. How do we get rid of our guilt, as individuals, as a community?"

As if the TV commercial hadn't been sleazy enough, now Butler was pitching his cars to the bishop? Isobel kept walking, tuning out the benediction and platitudes the bishop offered.

CHAPTER TWENTY

Sunday, June 20, noon

Kimberley came out of her house when Isobel pulled into the driveway. Isobel got out, saying, "Father Terrence called already?"

"What would make you ask a thing like that?"

Kimberley was giving her best butter-wouldn't-melt-in-her-mouth look, but Isobel wasn't sure whether that was because Father Terrence *had* already called, or because now Kimberley knew Isobel was going to want a favor.

"Out with it," Isobel said.

"With what?"

Fine. Two could play that game. "I'll be in the cottage if you need me."

She turned away.

"You're not even going to tell me what you were up to that would make Father Terrence call me?"

"If he called, I'm sure he already told you."

"Not really." Kimberley closed the distance between them. "Something about whether I'd asked for your help with Summerfest, and how proactive you seemed to be on that score."

Isobel hunched her shoulders. "What'd you tell him?"

"Haven't I always covered for you? I said I couldn't imagine trying to do everything myself this year, and it was so good of you to have volunteered to run errands for me."

Isobel exhaled and felt her shoulders relax.

"Now, are you going to tell me what errand it was I had you running, and why you didn't tell me about it beforehand?"

Nervously, Isobel looked around, even though she knew there was no way Michael—or anyone else—would overhear her. "I was looking for clues in Father Paul's office. I told Father Terrence I was looking for a copy of his notes for the opening prayer."

"Excellent!"

Isobel looked up at her friend. "Excellent?"

"You know I appreciate your cousin—mostly—but I think you stand a better chance of finding out what's going on than he does. Besides," Kimberley said, grinning, "Now you have to help me out by running errands so Father Terrence doesn't know you were lying to him. At least until your next confession."

Isobel's lips twitched at the reference to Michael's arrest of Kimberley the previous year, but her heart sank at her friend's final words. She hadn't even thought about confession! Maybe she'd see about visiting another parish?

"What kind of errands do you need run?"

"Why, did you have plans for this afternoon?"

"Greg is coming over. He might want to take me to some open houses—goodness knows the house-hunting with the real estate agent didn't work out well."

"Poor Richard. It's almost enough to make me sympathize with Sue. Almost."

Isobel snorted. "Given her attitude this morning when Momma and I went to drop off food for her, I wish I were as bad a cook as Michael says. She could use a good dose of food poisoning."

Kimberley's laugh was contagious. After a moment, though, Isobel sobered. "If someone had hit her over the head, I'd pin a medal on them. Richard's decent, though."

"Aside from his taste in women."

Isobel nodded; she'd thought the same herself recently. "That's always been true. You remember in high school—"

"You mean when he was already out of school but was dating Mr. Kilgore's daughter? Whatever happened to her?"

Kilgore had been the high school principal, and he hadn't been happy with his daughter dating someone older. The fact that she was past the legal age of consent only made it worse.

"She went to live with her grandparents out of state and finished up her degree by homeschooling, I think. For some reason, Momma wasn't keen on sharing the details with me."

"She wouldn't be." Kimberley got a gleam in her eye. "Maybe that's it! Richard's child has come back to town, determined to avenge the wrong done to his mother. Or her mother, I suppose."

"Not likely. If there is a child, he's not old enough to legally drive. And we'd have noticed if Martha Kilgore was swanning around town again."

"I suppose we would have." Kimberley's shoulders slumped. "Here I thought I'd cleverly solved the mystery and we could get back to ordinary life."

"Sorry to disappoint you," Isobel said. "Was there something you wanted me to do for you today?"

Kimberley gave a wicked grin. "I have a list."

Groaning, Isobel held her hand out. "Let's see it."

"I'll e-mail it to you. You don't have to get to it today. I'm not sure you can, anyway—it's things like verifying delivery with Sadie at the flower shop, collecting late fees, and verifying police presence with your cousin."

Sadie again. She'd been so *happy* to see Isobel the other day. Now she'd probably be even more snide. Richard had been nice to her, after all. With Isobel's luck, Sadie would accuse Isobel of having bashed Richard's head in. At least Sue hadn't gone that far.

Isobel didn't say any of that. "Michael will appreciate that. If I'm helping you, I'm not trying to do his job."

"I don't see why you can't do both at once."

"You're not my cousin."

"And thank goodness for that!"

Isobel had turned away, ready to go into her cottage and change into her yoga gear for a quick session before Greg came by, when Kimberley called her name again. "Isobel!"

She looked back over her shoulder to see Kimberley looking uncertain. She stopped. "What is it?"

Kimberley motioned to the steps leading to the side door. "Can we sit for a minute? There's something else I want to talk to you about."

Isobel followed her friend to the concrete steps and sat down close enough for her shoulder to brush against Kimberley's. Kimberley didn't speak right away, though, instead staring out at the small side yard, mostly driveway with a few forsythia bushes—incognito green this late in the year—edging it. The cottage, off to their left, had more cozy plantings around it, and both the cottage and garage had small amounts of gingerbread trim to match the house itself. Isobel felt the warm glow of home as she looked around.

"I keep trying to figure out the best way to tell you this," Kimberley finally said in a low voice. "It shouldn't be hard; we've always talked about everything."

Almost everything, but Isobel didn't correct her, just waited for Kimberley to say what was on her mind.

"They say you're not supposed to make major changes in the first year after your spouse dies—that your grief may drive you to decisions you'll later regret. I've been thinking about it, though, and I'm going to sell the house. It's too big for me on my own, and there are times my nerves still feel scraped raw." She leaned forward, covering her face with her hands. "I've been sleeping in the guest room for months. I need—something. To stop this, to make a clean break, to not have to face the thought of John every time I enter a room and think I catch a glimpse of something out of the corner of my eye. I need to get out."

Kimberley's shoulders started shaking. Isobel put her arm around Kimberley and held her until the sobs subsided. Kimberley looked up, dashed one hand across her eyes, and said, "Thanks."

"You needed it." Isobel cocked her head to one side. "I guess this means I should be looking for another rental." She rubbed her forehead. "With your house going on the market and Greg already out house-hunting, people are going to be even more likely to assume we'll be moving in together."

"You think tongues aren't wagging already?"

Isobel stuck her tongue out at Kimberley.

"Anyway, I'm not putting it up for sale right now, so you're safe for a little bit. I've got Summerfest to get through, and packing things up, then looking for somewhere else to live…I'd say at least a month or two. I would like to get it on the market this summer, though, if I can. Summer's prime moving season between families with children and people bound to the college calendar. If I don't sell it now, I might be stuck with it for another year."

Which, given her current nerves, wasn't a good option.

"Should I let Greg know you'll be selling? He might be interested."

Kimberley shook her head emphatically. "No. I wouldn't want to come back to visit you here. You understand, right?"

"Well, that's a little presumptuous of you."

Kimberley snorted. "You've been dating him for more than half a year, *and* he gets along with your mother. I'm amazed she hasn't booked the church already."

"Momma's not a true believer in love conquering all."

Sobering, Kimberley gave a wry smile. "No, I suppose she wouldn't be. Maybe I should be cynical, too, given all I learned about John, but I can't bring myself to feel that way. Betrayed? Yes. As though there's no hope for anyone? Nope. I think you two will be very happy together."

Isobel's face heated. She and Greg hadn't talked about anything long-term yet, never mentioned marriage. They did seem to take for granted that they would stay together—like when they were discussing Thanksgiving dinner, and he asked if he could have his parents there, too. No pressure, but a calm, quiet understanding. She thought they'd be happy together, too, but she wasn't about to say so.

Instead, she changed the subject. "You said 'come back to visit.' You just mean to the house, right? You're not leaving River Corners, are you?"

"Of course I'm staying here." Kimberley put her arms around Isobel. "This is home. I want to stay near my family, and it would be a pain moving the business."

"You want to stay near your best friend, too, right?"

"Oh, I don't know....She's a bit of a pain sometimes. Can you believe a *priest* called me to check up on her?"

"Well, you know how some of those priests can be—real busybodies, sticking their noses into everything."

"You'd *never* do that."

"Of course not."

They laughed together.

Isobel sobered first. "I hope that's not why Father Paul got killed. I could almost think he just looked into the pyramid the same way I did, out of curiosity, and he saw someone in there together that he wasn't supposed to see."

"Almost? That sounds rather reasonable to me, actually."

"It doesn't explain Richard, though, on the other side of town with the same putter."

"Did Michael tell you it was the same one?"

Isobel shook her head. "Michael didn't tell me anything except that he doesn't want me poking around and possibly getting attacked by a murderer again. You'd have a better chance getting information out of him than I would."

"Unlikely. He'd assume I was only asking so I could tell you."

"And he'd be right." Isobel stared at the steps for a minute, noting the imperfections at the edges, despite the careful upkeep. "Maybe I could ask Madge. She might tell me, even if Michael doesn't want her to."

"Oh, good, you're being devious again."

"Want to come with me to ask her?" Isobel hopped to her feet.

Kimberley arched an eyebrow. "I thought you were waiting for Greg to come over?"

"Oh, right." Isobel bit her lip. "I'll have to call her tomorrow and hope Michael doesn't hear me. Anyway, until I hear otherwise, I'm going to assume it's the same putter because one wasn't found with Father Paul's body, and I haven't heard of any other putters going missing."

"Which I assume you're also going to check out?"

"That would go over well, wouldn't it?" She mimed making a phone call. "'Excuse me, I'm the one who found the dead body in your pyramid. Could you tell me how many potential weapons you've misplaced lately?'"

Kimberley drew herself to her feet, much more gracefully than Isobel had. "I'm sure you'll think of a way to find out. Meanwhile, I've got to get back to working on the festival. Any chance you know someone on the college committee? I've had no luck finding out who they're going to get as a replacement chaplain."

"My boss is on the committee, and if she's representative of the rest of them, you're better off just making a decision and telling them what it is."

"Why are they on the committee if they don't care?"

"I'm sure they care, but they've got their own worries, too, and summer isn't the best time to get active participation from people at the college."

"It's never been a problem before. It's not like they have classes!"

Isobel shrugged. "Just bad timing this year." She wasn't going to mention Gerri's worries about the college budget to Kimberley, and if Gerri was that worried, it stood to reason others were as well. "I stick with what I said, though—just pick someone." She thought about the morning's homily. "Not the bishop. No one needs that kind of a downer to launch the festival. Maybe your good friend Father Terrence?"

The Miniature Golf Course Murders

"Should I let him know you recommended him?"

"He wouldn't believe you even if you did. But since you're going to have to call and ask him for Father Paul's notes, anyway—which, as I said, is what I told him I was looking for at your request—you can just ask him if he's found them, and either way, whether he'd be willing to give the opening prayer in Father Paul's place."

"That almost sounds reasonable."

"Sometimes, I can be." Isobel took a couple of steps backward. "I'll watch for your e-mail with my to-do list. Right now, though, I'm going to take a quick yoga break before Greg gets here."

"Good idea." Kimberley nodded solemnly. "It's always wise to stretch first."

CHAPTER TWENTY-ONE

Sunday, June 20, afternoon

Isobel twisted in the car seat to look at Greg. "So where are we going? Open houses, to hunt for both a home and a new agent at the same time?"

"Interesting idea. We might have to try that next weekend." He turned onto Main Street. "No, we're still owed eighteen holes of minigolf from the other day, and I thought we'd collect."

"And just happen to look for clues while we're there?"

"I wasn't planning to tell *them* that."

While they drove, Isobel filled Greg in on her morning's activity, including Father Terence catching her in Father Paul's office and his subsequent call to Kimberley to check her alibi.

"Excellent. Even more reason for you to poke around talking to suspects while you run her errands."

"I'm sure she thought of that," Isobel said dryly. "She thinks we're much more likely to solve this murder than Michael is."

"We've got a better track record."

The parking lot was packed, and Greg had trouble finding a spot. Finally, he settled for parking half on the verge and half on the edge of the lot itself. "Everyone wants to see the murder location, I guess."

"They didn't react like this at the Scotts' tree farm."

He held the door for her to get out. "That was scarier, more primal. We all hear tales of killers in the woods. Here, though, where everything's painted in primary colors and the sun is shining?" He shook his head. "Not one of these people is afraid that they're next on the list."

She slid out of her seat and walked with him to the entrance. "It doesn't seem fair. The Scotts are much nicer."

"Oh. It's you."

The rude greeting came from Tara O'Dell, Richard's receptionist, who stood behind the counter. She had said that Brian was her uncle, but Isobel still hadn't expected to run into her here.

Isobel pasted a smile on her face. "How nice to see you again. How are you holding up, with Richard in the hospital?"

Tara didn't return her smile. "I'll be fine. As if you care! Or that wife of his."

"Sue only cares about Sue, for the most part," Isobel agreed. "Although she did seem broken up earlier today when I saw her."

"Sure she was. If he dies, she loses the only thing that gives her any respect in this community. Why couldn't it have been her who was clobbered?"

"Too many suspects. No one much likes Sue, except for Sadie." Isobel ignored the bit about Sue having any respect. People might be polite to her for Richard's sake, but that didn't mean they actually respected her.

Tara ignored Isobel's words of solidarity. "Can I help you with something?"

Yes, but given the girl's attitude, Isobel didn't hold out much hope. "Is your uncle here?"

"He's too busy to talk to anyone." Her favorite refrain. No wonder Brian had her running interference today; she had lots of practice at it.

Greg stepped in, leaning on the counter so he was eye-to-eye with Tara. He smiled, and his voice dropped just a touch. "We'd really appreciate it if you told him we were here. We'd like to finish our round from the other day."

She jerked her head sideways, an emphatic no, and motioned to a sign on the wall. "We're not responsible for incomplete games. You'll have to pay, just like everyone else."

He pulled his receipt from the other day out of his shirt pocket and turned it over to show the reverse side. "According to your rules, any game that is paid for but not begun can be played any time within a week. That means we have the eighteen-hole game still available."

Unimpressed by his logic, Tara sniffed. "I have only your word for it that you didn't start that game."

"Right." Isobel couldn't contain her sarcasm. "Because after we found the dead body, we went ahead and started playing the other course before deciding to report it."

"You might have. My uncle told me you didn't even tell him what was going on. Why should I believe you any more than he did?"

"Yes, I know he didn't believe me. That worked out well for him, didn't it?"

Greg straightened up and turned toward her, a warning look on his face. "Isobel…"

"Look, either give us the game, or get us your uncle," Isobel said to Tara.

"How are you going to make me?"

Isobel smiled sweetly. "Did you know that the city has very strict rules about moonlighting? I'd be willing to bet your boss didn't sign off on the paperwork for you." She raised her hand to her mouth. "Oops. And he can't now, can he? It would be a shame if he got out of the hospital and found he had to start interviewing for a new receptionist."

"Shows what you know. I'm not getting paid for this."

Isobel hadn't thought she was, any more than Kimberley had gotten paid by Sadie the other day for watching the flower shop. Where Sadie owned the shop, though, Brian was only a manager and could get in trouble with his boss for letting someone unauthorized handle the money.

"Really? So if I were to, say, text Ms. Metzger in Hawaii, she'd know about this arrangement?"

"That's blackmail."

Isobel shrugged. She was saved from answering by the office door behind Tara opening. Brian O'Dell came out, wearing what appeared to be the same polo shirt he'd had on the other day—although he might well have one for every day of the week, Isobel supposed.

"Tara, what I have told you about arguing with the customers?"

"They're trying to get a free game!"

Greg said, "No. According to the rules printed on the receipts, we're still owed a game on the back course."

Brian nodded. "He's right. Give them the score card and putters. And try to be less confrontational."

He turned to go back in to the office.

Tara said, "But—"

"No buts," he said. "You don't want me to talk to your father about this."

Tara swallowed. Any sympathy Isobel felt for her vanished, however, when Tara gave them a vindictive look. "They're going to have to share a putter. All the other ones are out already."

"And we're one shy. Fine. Just do it." The door closed behind him.

Outside on the course, Isobel rolled her eyes. "Could she be any more unhelpful?"

"Don't ask. I'm sure she'd try." Greg picked out a bright orange ball. "I watched her while you were talking about the mayor. It wouldn't surprise me at all to find that he was having a fling with her. She's certainly possessive enough."

Isobel snorted. "Not even his taste in women could be that bad twice. I'm fairly certain it's unrequited."

He motioned her to precede him to the first hole, an obstacle course of concrete carpets with ripples and holes set up to look like a flying carpet shop. "I notice you didn't say he'd never cheat on Sue."

"After John? I don't think I can judge that, although it's safe to say no one in town would think badly of him for it. Except maybe Sadie." She thought about it as she lined up her first shot. "No, definitely Sadie. With her own divorce and Sue being her only close friend left, she'd be yelling about it from the rooftops."

"Or passing judgement with a golf club over his head?"

She thought about that while waiting for Greg to take his swing. They ended up on opposite sides of the hole, roughly equidistant, although she'd have to go up and down three carpet ridges to take the shortest shot to the hole. Not exactly a sure thing.

"She might. In fact, Sadie's the only one I can see with a motive to kill both Father Paul and Richard, but she was broken up when I stopped in to her shop the other day."

"Guilty conscience?" His ball dropped into the hole.

"I don't think so. I think there's something we're still overlooking."

They went through the next three holes without discussing the murder or attempted murder. Isobel groaned when Greg got a hole in one on the third hole, and he complimented her on the fourth hole when she came in one stroke under par. As they waited for the trio ahead of them at the fifth hole, Greg motioned for Isobel to follow him then led the way to the fence.

Isobel stared at the gap in the chain-link. "I'm surprised anyone pays for games with this here. It's like an open invitation."

"If you can get to it, sure," Greg said. "But you'd have to be at the car lot or parked on the street to use it. People would notice."

"Or maybe at the house across the street. Brian said there'd been people there. I forgot to ask Momma if she knew anything about it, though. She told me all about the people who moved out of the first house we looked at yesterday."

"Good thought. If anybody knows anything, it's going to be her. Or your Aunt Rosa."

"Do you know how much trouble I'd get in if I asked Aunt Rosa instead of Momma?"

He chuckled instead of answering.

Isobel glanced from the fence to the pyramid in the front course. By absolute distance, only the hole they were playing was closer. If someone wanted to leave in a hurry—say, after committing a murder—they could climb the shorter fence between the two sections, slip through the chain-link, and vanish. They'd need somewhere to vanish *to*, however.

"You know? Maybe I do need to shop for a new car."

"Can I test drive the convertible?"

"Don't be ridiculous. If I'm shopping, *I* get to test drive it."

Greg gave a longing sigh as he stared at the blue convertible. "Can I at least get to drive it sometimes?"

"We'll see."

She didn't have any intention of buying the convertible. As she'd said, it wasn't practical. Window shopping would be fun, though, and would give them a chance to find out what Butler had noticed the day of the murder.

Greg led the way back to the hole, which had been free for a couple of minutes now. "Michael's not going to be fooled."

She shrugged. "He can't prove anything."

"He could lock you in the back of his car again until you confess."

"Remind me to put an air-freshener in my messenger bag, just in case."

CHAPTER TWENTY-TWO

Monday, June 21, morning

Isobel was still turning over their visit to the minigolf course the next morning as she walked to work. She wished she knew what Michael had found out, but where he would have dropped by her place to talk in the past, he hadn't been as frequent a visitor of late. He and Violet did make a cute couple, though.

She hesitated on the edge of the town square. Just as Richard had said, the shops around the square had their sidewalk sale signs out to draw in customers, even though the festival itself didn't start until Wednesday. Two more days—no wonder Kimberley wanted help with errands and loose ends.

Work was south; the police station was north. Isobel had a lot to do even without the errands she'd promised she'd take care of for her friend—she was expecting the ghostwriter to check in with a first estimate on Enzian's manuscript—and Gerri wouldn't approve of Isobel spending time chasing a murderer when the Board might be looking for any reason to cut their budget. Michael didn't want her involved, either. Good sense told her she should turn and go to work.

No one ever accused her of having common sense, however. She headed for the police station.

Instead of going to her cousin's office, after signing in she went down the stairs to the coroner's office and forensics department. A chemical smell, with strong overtones of bleach and formaldehyde, lay on the air. Madge's door was open, but Isobel tapped on the door frame.

Madge pushed her stringy hair back from her face and looked up from the paperwork she was filling out. "Does your cousin know you're here?"

Isobel stepped inside. "Only if he's looked at the register this morning."

"You trying to get me in trouble with my boss?"

"We both know if he gets unhappy at anyone, it's going to be me."

Madge snorted. "I can't believe you said *if*."

"Okay, when."

Madge hadn't gotten any visitors' chairs since the last time Isobel had been down this way; she probably didn't get many people who wanted to stick around. Isobel settled for bracing herself on the corner of Madge's desk, one hip propped up while the other leg dangled free.

"You know I can't comment on an on-going investigation."

"You make it sound like I'm a reporter. I was just curious…"

"Uh-huh."

"I'm always curious." Isobel tried to think about where to go from there, when she was interrupted by a voice from the doorway.

"What are you doing here?"

Isobel popped off the corner of Madge's desk, wondering whether there was anything she could hide behind as her cousin strode up to her. He looked even less happy than he had the previous day at church.

"Didn't I tell you to stay out of it?" Michael towered over her, inches away, forcing her to look up at him.

"I saw the newspaper editorial this morning, thought maybe you could use a friendly ear."

"Thanks. I'm good." He took a step back and pointed her to the door. "You've done your charitable act for the day, and we can both get some work done now."

"Good? They're pillorying you, and even Momma said nice things about Sue Holstein."

The apparent non sequitur didn't seem to bother Michael; neither of their mothers ever said nice things about Sue, so this was serious. The glare slipped from his face, and Isobel noticed the shadows under his eyes; he hadn't been sleeping. "Richard's popular. We're just fortunate he wasn't killed."

"Is he going to be okay?"

He nodded, once. "He woke up about five this morning. I headed up to Majors to see him, but he refuses to talk."

"You're kidding! Does he realize somebody tried to kill him?"

The Miniature Golf Course Murders

"I asked him the same thing. Doesn't matter. He's not talking."

"Idiot," Madge put in. Isobel glanced around, surprised. She'd almost forgotten Madge's presence, even though this was her office.

Michael agreed. "He's had state troopers guarding his room since he was brought in, but when the hospital releases him, it's going to be much harder to keep him safe."

Isobel brightened. "Ooh, can we get a cliché? The murderer sneaks into Richard's hotel room to silence him, but it's a trap?"

Michael shook his head. "You've watched too many TV dramas."

"Are you telling me it wouldn't work?"

"Yes, Isobel, that's exactly what I'm telling you. His attacker isn't dumb—no fingerprints, no telltale hairs, nothing left at the scene that matches anything from Father Paul's death."

"Except the putter," Isobel said. "Brian said they were only missing the one."

He scowled at her again. "You were poking around there again?"

"Not exactly." Isobel stared down at the tile floor, noting absently that two of the tiles had been set at a ninety degree angle to the others, making their streaks stand out. "Greg and I wanted to play the game that we didn't get to the other day. We had to share a putter."

"Oh, the tragedy!"

She stuck her tongue out at him. "They were really busy, so all the other putters were out. Not that Tara wanted us to have even that one."

"Who's Tara?"

"Brian's niece, who was working the counter for him. She's also Richard's receptionist, and she doesn't like me much. She didn't want to let me in to talk to him the other day."

"I must remember to send her flowers," Michael said.

"Beast. I suppose she let you right in?"

"Well, no," he admitted. "It seems to be a family trait, this lack of cooperation. O'Dell hadn't even told us for sure how many putters were missing."

Isobel couldn't help it. She grinned. She had known something Michael didn't.

He noticed the grin, and his eyebrows lowered farther. "That doesn't mean I want you poking around. Right now, I'm operating on the assumption that

Richard saw something when he was at the minigolf course the other day—or at least that someone thought he saw something—and that's why he was targeted. We're looking for other connections Father Paul and Richard had, like they're both in Rotary, but so far this is the best we've got for motivation."

"What's that have to do with me poking around?"

"Someone hit both of them over the head with the putter—someone they saw coming. If that someone thinks you know something…"

She sighed. She got the point, but—"Really? They were hit from the front? So it was someone they knew."

"That narrows it down," Madge said. "There must be, oh, all of six people in town who don't know them both."

Michael snorted. "It's higher than that, but that's the basic problem. Everyone's a suspect."

"Even me?" Isobel forced her eyes wide.

"Maybe not you." He stared down at her for a moment, his face deadly serious. "If you hit someone over the head with a minigolf putter, I'd assume it was because your skill hasn't improved any since you were a teen."

Madge laughed, and Isobel put her hands on her hips. "It's amazing you haven't managed to scare off Greg yet, with all the mean things you say about me."

He shrugged. "I warned Stone he was taking his life into his hands. If he wants to ignore me, that's his prerogative."

"Hmph." They were back to their normal banter. Life was good. "I just wish we'd made time to go poking around at the house across the way from the course."

"Don't bother," he said. "The people O'Dell saw there earlier this year were hired by the Heming heirs to fix the place up. They didn't say anything about when they're planning on moving in, but there's nothing suspicious about the people there."

"Darn."

"Isobel, give up. Go to work. I know you have things to do. Let me do my job, which includes keeping my bull-headed cousin out of danger even when she deliberately courts it. You really don't want Madge here telling me all about the murder weapon that was used to bash in your head."

"It wouldn't be a putter at least." Isobel tried to lighten the mood.

It didn't work.

The Miniature Golf Course Murders

"I really don't think Aunt Maria Elena would care, do you?"

CHAPTER TWENTY-THREE

Monday, June 21, lunch time

The door next to the flower shop opened onto a narrow flight of stairs leading to the second floor. At the top, a similarly narrow hallway led the width of the building, with two doors to either side. An elevator had been clumsily grafted opposite the stairs, allowing access to those who had trouble negotiating stairs. The first door on the left stood open, and Isobel stepped inside.

Windows on the far wall gave a panoramic view of the town square. From her desk on the right-hand wall where she could keep an eye on the door and look out the windows, Kimberley glowered at Isobel. "I was beginning to think you weren't coming. The receipt book is here, and there's a copy of what fees are still owed. Don't let anyone tell you they owe a different amount."

"Sorry. Lots to do at work, and I was a bit late getting in this morning." Isobel dropped her messenger bag on the small table next to the door. She wanted to relax for a minute before rushing off on Kimberley's errands.

"Minigolf kept you out late?"

"No!" Isobel felt heat rushing to her face. "Nothing like that. I stopped off at the police station this morning to poke around a bit."

"I'll bet Michael loved that."

"Not so much. I got another lecture on him not wanting to tell my mother that my head had been bashed in." Isobel thought about that for a minute. "That's not precisely the way he put it, but the end message was the same: butt out, stop poking in things that don't concern you, do your job and let me do mine."

"The usual, in other words." Kimberley made a note on the pad in front of her, then glanced up again. "I don't suppose you thought to confirm police presence for Summerfest with him while you had him cornered?"

"No, I can honestly say that didn't cross my mind."

"Then you're going to have to talk to him again."

Isobel hesitated. "He gave me the definite impression he didn't want to see me at the police station again."

"Then call him." Kimberley looked sympathetic. "I know, I know—he's going to think you're trying to pump him for more information about the murder and the attack on Richard. Tell him up front you're helping me tie up loose ends. I've only got two more days, and you wouldn't believe the number of things that I still have to deal with."

"I'd say better you than me, but I'm pretty sure that I agreed to take some of them on."

"You can relax when it's over."

"Isn't that usually my line?" Isobel crossed to Kimberley's desk and picked up the receipt book and fee schedule. "Looks pretty straightforward. I printed out a copy of the invoice to double-check with Sadie, too, so I'll probably start there." She grinned. "Since she *is* so close." Then she hesitated. "Wait—given that she is just downstairs, why do you need me to talk to her? You see her all the time."

Kimberley cocked her head to one side and raised her eyebrows, as if waiting for Isobel to catch up with a conversation. Isobel just shook her head.

"Because you're supposed to be poking around, remember?" Kimberley said with some asperity.

"I can't very well tell her that if she asks why you didn't just talk to her!"

"I'm spending the day chasing down Health Department permits, verifying that everyone has provided proof of insurance and signed all the waivers, and trying to find out why there's an entire section of tents that has yet to be delivered."

"Okay, then." Isobel tapped the receipt book against her palm, casting through her thoughts for any other questions she had. She couldn't come up with any. Oh, wait—"Can I just e-mail Michael to ask about the police presence for you? He doesn't get nearly as annoyed with me in print."

Kimberley chuckled. "That's fine. A good idea, actually, because I like having everything written down if possible. Makes it easier to point out to others when things aren't going according to plan."

"All right. I'd better get moving—I'm taking a long lunch, then I'll work late again. Violet said the doctor okayed her to come in for a few hours this afternoon and tomorrow, and I want to be there when she gets in."

"So you can catch her when she faints at the mountains of work waiting for her?"

"Something like that. Or at least to act as a buffer so Gerri doesn't try to overwork her."

As Isobel stepped out of the door downstairs, she bumped into a wheeled cart full of Gerbera daisies.

"Watch where you're going!" Sadie snapped.

"I'm sorry, but you're blocking the door." Isobel kept her voice calm. "I'm being as careful as I can."

"Nonsense!" But Sadie rolled the cart half a yard closer to her own door before locking the wheels again. She glanced over at Isobel. "How's your new plant doing?"

"I haven't managed to kill it yet. I think it might like my office." Isobel changed the subject. "I'm running errands for Kimberley, for Summerfest. Do you have time to go over the order and delivery confirmation now?"

Sadie rolled her eyes and gave a loud groan. "I suppose. Kimberley told me this morning as she was coming in that she had dozens of loose ends to chase down today and tomorrow. I was thinking they might wind up canceling the opening prayer."

"The chaplain's one of the loose ends," Isobel agreed. As far as she knew, Kimberley hadn't asked Father Terrence yet. "And with Richard in the hospital, goodness only knows who will be there at the opening ceremonies besides Kimberley."

"Maybe she could ask Sue? Sue doesn't have any official position with the city, but…"

The suggestion made sense. River Corners didn't have a deputy mayor to step in, and if Kimberley asked anyone from the City Council, there would be in-fighting for weeks afterward about how the selection was made. As little love as Isobel had for Sue, the mayor's wife was a reasonable choice to fill in for him.

And it would thrill Sue no end to finally get some level of official recognition—especially if Kimberley had to ask for her help.

"That's a good idea. I'll pass it on to Kimberley." Isobel reached into her messenger bag and pulled out the printouts of the floral orders. "Now, about this paperwork."

It took twenty minutes to go through all the printouts, verify that the orders were correct, that everything that needed to be shipped from out of town was on its way, and that the flowers would be in place by seven o'clock Wednesday morning.

As Isobel was about to leave, she paused. "What did you do with the petition you had the other day? The one to eliminate the opening prayer?"

Sadie flushed. "Just when I thought you might actually be decent, you go and bring that up. Can't we drop it? The man is dead."

"Yes, he is, and it's possible that anyone who signed that petition might hold a grudge against him for some other reason."

The color abruptly drained from Sadie's face, taking all of her anger with it. "You mean the murderer might have signed my petition?" She cast a sidelong look at the recycling bin tucked in the back corner of the shop. "But they couldn't have been at the campus and at the minigolf course at the same time, could they?"

Isobel ignored the singular *they*. It made at least as much sense as *he or she*. "I'm sure we weren't the only people you caught leaving campus, and I imagine there were some people just passing by who signed it."

Sadie licked her lips. "You don't think the murderer will come after me, do you? Since I might be able to point a finger at them?"

She hadn't meant to scare Sadie. "You'll probably be okay. Your shop is right on the square. Everyone can see you here."

"I have to go home sometime."

Isobel felt a stab of sympathy for Sadie. Michael might believe Isobel didn't care about her own well-being, but she remembered the feeling when her home had been broken into the previous winter and how she'd jumped at shadows even after Jennifer had been arrested. She didn't want to see Sadie go through that.

"Call the police. Have them send someone over to pick up the petition. If the killer knows that the police already have all the information you can give them, maybe you'll be left alone."

"Maybe?"

Isobel shrugged helplessly. "I can't promise anything. All I can do is suggest that you make it as public as possible."

Sadie grinned wryly. "I think I can do that. I'll skip the Five-and-Diner this time, though."

Who would have guessed that Sadie could laugh about that? Waving, Isobel headed out to start hitting the names on Kimberley's list. Momma's name wasn't on it; she'd probably paid all of her fees the day she decided to participate. Just as well—if Isobel had to stop by Momma's, there was no way she was getting back to work this afternoon. As it was, she was going to have to grab a pre-made sandwich from the corner store instead of sitting down to eat at the diner.

CHAPTER TWENTY-FOUR

Monday, June 21, afternoon

Violet was already at her desk by the time Isobel got back. She nodded at the sandwich in Isobel's hand. "Did you bring enough to share?"

Isobel hefted the sandwich. "You can have it. I'll just grab something from the vending machine. I think they just restocked the Bugles."

Her assistant laughed. "You are so easy. I ate before I came in, silly. Any new crises to deal with today?"

Dropping her messenger bag into the lower drawer of her desk, Isobel shook her head. "Nothing new, just the same old ones piling up. The ghostwriter is hard at work on Enzian's manuscript, made harder by the fact that Enzian doesn't want to actually talk to the ghostwriter about what it is he wants to say. A couple of authors are being slow in returning their copyedits, and I had to send them reminder e-mails that if I don't hear from them, I'll have to just accept the copyedits and proceed so the books will make their print dates. You know, the usual."

"At least we're not getting poems in the slush?"

"There is that."

Isobel dropped into her chair and propped her feet up on her still-open drawer. She unwrapped the sandwich and took a bite. The horseradish was pretty bland, but the roast beef was tasty enough. She chewed thoughtfully. She hadn't found out anything while running around for Kimberley except that Sadie was actually human. Not exactly a stop-the-presses revelation.

"I know something new." Violet kept her eyes on her monitor as though deeply engrossed in her work. Her tone didn't sound like she was discussing manuscripts, though. "Or at least new to you."

"And just what do you know?"

"Our boss is on Michael's list of suspects. It seems she wasn't actually in the meeting she said she was the day Father Paul was killed."

"I don't blame her. Committee meetings are dull as dirt." As Isobel had discovered firsthand on Thursday.

"Doesn't explain where she was."

But there hadn't been a committee meeting Wednesday…Gerri had been here in the office, complaining about the spreadsheets and the numbers, even coming in to demand the files a second time. Unless that was just her way of creating an alibi for herself?

Isobel chewed thoughtfully. If Gerri hadn't mentioned her break-up, Isobel would have thought she was just sneaking off for some time with Len. Maybe she'd found someone new? Or not found someone yet, but was looking? She certainly wouldn't want to talk about a first date with the police. "Oh, sure, here's who I was with. He'll vouch that I wasn't committing a murder."

On the other hand, the last time there had been murders around town, it had been someone from the college. It could have happened again. Talk about your town-gown divide!

"So what motive does Michael think she has?"

Violet shrugged. "He didn't say. He might not even think she's really a suspect."

"Then why was he checking out her alibi? Why did she even have to provide one? He's not going door-to-door for the whole town, is he?"

Violet gave her an innocent glance. "Would you believe me if I told you he was checking your alibi?"

Isobel couldn't help it; she laughed, then grabbed a napkin to clean up the bits of sandwich she had sprayed. "Try again."

"He wanted to know if I had homework I was supposed to be doing?"

It was a good thing Isobel hadn't taken another bite from her sandwich. She would have choked on that for sure. As it was, she snorted.

"Okay. The truth is, Gerri lives next door to Saint Theresa's, and sometimes people park in front of her house when they're running late. She's been heard yelling at both priests about cars blocking her driveway."

It was a topic that came up frequently in the announcements and the bulletin—at least once a month, there was a plea to be courteous to others and mindful of where you parked. Michael knew that as well as Isobel did, but it didn't seem like the sort of thing one would kill over. Shooting the person who left their car in front of Gerri's driveway so she couldn't get out? Maybe, although Isobel wouldn't have pegged Gerri as that sort of person. Killing the priest who tried to discourage people from doing it? That didn't make any sense at all.

She said as much, and Violet shrugged. "He has to check it out. *Somebody* did it, after all."

Yes, somebody had killed the priest, and it didn't sound like Michael was any closer to figuring out who it was—which was probably why he'd been so upset at her poking around this morning. Isobel was willing to take any lead she could get, though, and it would be easy for her to check out their boss's office. Not right this minute; Violet would almost certainly tell Michael what Isobel was up to.

She'd need a pretext to visit Gerri's office, and she might have one. She'd asked Gerri twice by e-mail for copies of her correspondence with Enzian, so Isobel would have a complete file, but so far Gerri had ignored her request.

An hour later, Isobel called Gerri's office and received no answer. Perfect! She excused herself to take a bathroom break—and sailed past the women's room to Gerri's office.

Isobel paused in the doorway. Gerri might be back at any minute, and if she found Isobel here, she wasn't going to be pleased. In for a penny, in for a pound. She stepped inside.

Gerri's office was obsessively neat. A framed picture of Gerri's parents with Gerri as a young child sat atop the beige file cabinet against the left wall. The right wall was filled with floor-to-ceiling bookshelves, with reference books in the section next to Gerri's desk that was neatly marked off by a border of blue tape. The rest of the shelves were filled with copies of books the press had produced. No other decorations distracted from the central desk with its ergonomically correct angles and computer.

No, that wasn't quite true—a piece of paper lay next to Gerri's keyboard. Isobel sat down in Gerri's chair and looked over the note. Short, handwritten—and surrounded by doodles in green gel ink. The doodles were obviously Gerri's handiwork—she wouldn't use any other color, said that authors found it to be friendly—while the note itself was written in anonymous black ink. The signature, though, made it less than anonymous—Len, Gerri's ex.

Isobel peered at the cramped handwriting. "Meet me tomorrow at the usual place."

She couldn't be certain when the note had been written—was this something that was months old, or had Gerri found it in her campus mailbox this morning?

Gerri had said they broke up over Christmas—and the anguish in her voice had seemed real enough. Maybe he wanted to get back together with her? The note gave no hint of a reason. All Isobel had to go on was that Gerri had held onto the note and decorated it with both hearts and daggers. Some mixed emotions there.

The fact that it was sitting on the desk when everything else was tucked neatly away—including the green pen Gerri had used for the doodles—implied that it was recent. Isobel wondered where the usual place was, and how Gerri was expected to know what time to show up.

She shook her head. Interesting, this might be, but it had nothing to do with whether Gerri had—or needed—an alibi for Father Paul's death. Where else should she look?

"Did you need something?" Gerri's voice was chillier than Isobel had ever heard it, but she didn't blame her boss.

She looked up to see her boss standing in the doorway, her glare even icier than her voice had been.

"I was looking to see if you had copies of your interactions with Mr. Enzian. He harangued me for forty-five minutes this morning about how he didn't have time to answer questions and he still didn't understand why if you had accepted his manuscript it couldn't be printed as is. I figured it would help if he tells me, 'Your boss said…' if I could see what you had actually said. Since his opinion of the press is so important."

The words rolled off her tongue easily; it was a good thing she'd practiced her excuse. She knew her voice probably sounded snide at the end, but Isobel couldn't help it. Anyone who couldn't see why copying entire chapters of other people's work was wrong shouldn't have the right to pass judgement on her work. Shouldn't be employed by an academic institution, either, but that wasn't her call to make.

"You could have e-mailed me." Gerri's voice hadn't warmed up any.

"I did. Twice. I also tried calling, but you didn't answer."

"It didn't occur to you that I have other things to do and I'd get to your problem when I had time?"

"It occurred to me that I had other things to do last week when you insisted I waste an entire afternoon sitting in a meeting where I had nothing to contribute. It occurred to me that I didn't have time to listen to him tell me how precious his time is. It occurred to me that I wouldn't even be in this situation if you had the sense to tell him how bad a shape the manuscript was in and how much work it would need when you overruled my rejection." Isobel took a deep breath. "It also occurs to me that maybe I'm tired of picking up all the slack around here. Maybe you should look for a new managing editor who figures that part of her job description is doormat because you sure don't seem to appreciate the one you have."

Where had that come from? She wasn't interested in looking for another job, and Momma would have a fit if Isobel left River Corners. Besides, as Kimberley had said about herself, everything and almost everyone Isobel cared for lived was here. She wasn't about to apologize, though.

"If you leave now, I'll forget that you said this," Gerri said. "I'm in a good mood today—mostly—and willing to let this slide. I'll photocopy the information you need and leave it in your mailbox."

A good mood? No doubt because of the note from Len. It was recent, then.

Isobel stood, lifted her chin, and walked past Gerri wordlessly.

She'd noticed before that when she most owed someone an apology was when she felt the most righteous indignation. That need to justify herself. What she'd said about her time was true, but that really didn't excuse her ransacking Gerri's office looking for clues. She hadn't even gotten anything worth the trouble—just the knowledge that Gerri might be seeing Len again. Really useful.

CHAPTER TWENTY-FIVE

Monday, June 21, evening

Isobel stepped through her door, dropped her bag, and slumped in her favorite horseshoe chair. She'd talked to everybody today—including Michael, who wouldn't have approved of the rest of her day at all—and she didn't feel any nearer to finding out who the killer was. As soon as she had the energy, she was going to go crawl into her tub and not come out until she was a prune.

Her stomach rumbled. Perhaps she should eat something first. And she should call Greg. She didn't have anything to report about the day, but talking to him made her feel better. Just thinking about him lifted her spirits, and she reached for her cellphone.

Unfortunately, he didn't answer.

She frowned. He'd said he was going to be packing more boxes tonight, hadn't he? He might be busy, or he could have stepped out for a minute. He might even have a mouthful of food. She'd try again in a little bit. Meanwhile, she'd get herself something to eat.

Her refrigerator wasn't quite bare—she still had the dough for the cinnamon rolls she hadn't baked this weekend—but all of the food her mother had given her was gone. Thank goodness for breakfast leftovers from the Farmhouse.

Maybe she would go ahead and bake up the cinnamon rolls. They'd be a decent dessert, and she could take the extras into work in the morning. Okay, roll out the dough first. Or no, get together the filling first—unsalted butter, brown sugar, cinnamon, nutmeg—ooh, and some chopped nuts would be good.

Fifteen minutes later, the cinnamon rolls were cut and rising in the pan, and the oven was preheating to bake them. Now she was really hungry, and she zapped her leftovers in the microwave and sat back down in the horseshoe chair. She glanced at the tottering pile of books beside her, trying to decide whether to grab something to read while she ate. She hadn't had much chance to read over the past week. The top half dozen all clamored for her attention, though. Worse than not having anything to read was having too much to read and not knowing where to start; it definitely contributed to her tsundoku habit. One of these years, though, she was going to get to all of these unread books.

Just not today.

Next time she had leftovers from the Farmhouse—assuming there was a next time, which given their portion sizes seemed likely—she'd have to remember to reheat them in the oven instead of the microwave. Both the waffle and the egg white were rubbery. The oven might not help with the egg, but it would keep the waffle crisper, she was certain. The food was still delicious, even if the texture was off. She polished off the last of the food and washed the plate before sliding the cinnamon rolls into the oven.

She tried Greg's cell again, but it still went to his voice mail.

"Hi, it's me. Just wanted to catch you up on all the running around I've been doing today. You'd think with the number of people I've talked to, I'd actually know who the killer is by now, but nooo." She sighed. "Give me a call back when you get in. I love hearing your voice."

She hung up. Had she actually said that? They'd just been out yesterday afternoon. And Saturday morning. He was going to think she was desperate!

A bath really would be good. She'd just need to start it scalding hot since she wouldn't be getting in just yet. It should be just the right temperature to slip into after the cinnamon rolls came out of the oven. Meanwhile, she could make a list of everything she knew and what questions she still had.

When the oven beeped for her to take out the cinnamon rolls, she put her pen down next to her notepad. The list of things she knew was so far confined to the obvious: Father Paul was dead, Richard had been attacked, the same person had probably attacked them both, and the same weapon was used. In other words, pretty much what everyone else knew or suspected.

There were a few details—like the sawdust Madge had mentioned, or the fact that only a single putter had been taken—most likely the one Father Paul had been using on the course—that bore mentioning. She thought about it while she took the cinnamon rolls out to cool.

"Maybe it was Sue," she said aloud. "Father Paul wouldn't think she was a threat, and it would explain why Richard won't say anything."

She glanced toward her bathroom longingly. The bath would have to wait—and it would most likely be cold by the time she got back. She sighed and headed out the door.

Kimberley called, "Come in," when Isobel knocked on the side door. Inside, she sat at one of the long banquet tables she used for crafting, ticking items off on a list.

"What do you think of Sue?" she started.

Kimberley looked amused. "Do we really have time to go into that now? I think we both know exactly what I think about her."

Isobel chuckled. "Okay, that was a little vague. I meant, do you think she could be the murderer? Richard would never tell if it was her."

"Lots of motive," Kimberley agreed. "She could have offed Father Paul for her friend Sadie, and then attacked Richard when he figured out what was going on. There's just one problem."

"What's that?"

"When Father Paul was getting killed, Sue was in Sadie's shop, haranguing me about why I should let her help out with Summerfest because evidently, she doesn't think anyone cares about that old nepotism law, and she said so at great length."

Isobel perched on a second banquet table, across from Kimberley. This one was relatively free of papers, and she didn't think she'd mess up anything. "She says everything at great length."

"There is that," Kimberley said drily. "But it doesn't change the fact that she's got an alibi."

"Darn."

CHAPTER TWENTY-SIX

Tuesday, June 22

Isobel chewed on her red pen. The printer's e-mail said that two spaces had opened up in their calendar, and did she have something she wanted to move up? She had three titles that might be ready on time, but she knew from experience that the one author always took an extra week reviewing his copyedits. He'd love the earlier press date, but there was no way he would meet it. She sent e-mails to the indexers that she'd scheduled for the other two projects and asked if they could meet the earlier deadline, presuming the same amount of time to work?

"I don't think there is much nutritional value in plastic." Greg leaned against the door frame, watching her.

She took the pen out of her mouth. "I'm saving my calories for the festival tomorrow. Funnel cakes, hot dogs, cotton candy, Momma's cookies…"

"Ah, pre-dieting."

"I've also been snacking on cinnamon rolls." She pointed to the three left next to the water pot.

"You did make them after all. I'll have to try one." He straightened up. "I found a place I'm thinking of putting an offer on. Want to come see?"

When had he had time to look? He must have been busy while she'd been running errands and snooping. Or maybe when she'd tried to reach him the previous night.

She cast a guilty glance at Violet.

Violet made shooing motions with her hands. "Go. I was planning to work late tonight to catch up anyway." She frowned at her inbox. "Well, start to catch up. Michael's going to come by with take-out later. Just give me a call and tell me all about it when you get home."

Isobel didn't need a second invitation. She put her computer to sleep, grabbed her messenger bag from the desk drawer where she stored it, and headed out the door.

"So where is it?" Isobel asked as they walked to Greg's car.

He finished off the cinnamon roll in his hand before answering. "It's a surprise." He grinned at her. "I want to see whether you can figure it out before we actually get there."

She rolled her eyes and shook her head. All right, a challenge was a challenge.

Greg drove east along Main Street. Isobel frowned. There hadn't been much new development this direction. He was either looking at something older, or he'd found something in the next town over. She felt a sinking feeling inside. She didn't want him that far away.

He slowed as they approached the minigolf emporium.

"I thought we were looking at a house, not golfing."

"We are." He grinned triumphantly, signaling to turn left.

"The Heming place?" Even though Michael had said it was being fixed up, it wouldn't have occurred to her to have Greg look at it.

"No points for figuring it out this late."

The packed-dirt drive wove behind some trees. Around the bend, the yard opened up. The grass hadn't been mowed this summer, and feathery stalks waved in the breeze. Bushes and trees showed evidence of having been trimmed back to shape, probably in the spring. What really drew they eye, though, was the house.

The Hemings had been one of the earliest families in River Corners, and succeeding generations had expanded the house to meet current aesthetics. The resulting home was a mélange of styles, with dormers mixing with oriel and eyebrows windows, a tower on the left side of the house, and a large porch with Doric columns. The roof looked like it might have Mansard roots, but it had changed with time, although it was still covered with actual slate shingles.

The drive curved around to the back, but Greg stopped the car in front of the double front doors.

Isobel got out of the car and stared up at the house. "It's...big."

"Brian was right. The heirs were fixing it up. Everything's been updated—wiring, plumbing, central heat and air." He led her up the steps and across the porch. A lockbox hung on the front door, and he freed the key from inside.

From the exterior, she had been expecting a grand entryway. There wasn't one; the front door opened directly into the living room. Open doors led off to either side, and a wooden staircase arced up to the second floor. This must have been the original home, the core that everything else had been built off of.

"They refinished the hardwood, but they didn't replace anything."

Wordlessly, Isobel stepped away from him, peering through the open door on the right. Inside was a cozy room lined with wooden bookcases and windows—not quite as picture perfect as the one in the new subdivision, but much warmer and homelike. She could easily see Greg settling in here to grade papers.

Further investigation showed the kitchen to the rear of the house with a door that led out to the garage. "You'll want to cover that walkway," Isobel said.

The door on the left led to the tower. The bottom floor was large enough for a sitting room, and a wrought-iron staircase spiraled up around the edge. She followed it up at least two stories and caught her breath. Only one window looked to the front of the property, but glass lined the other three sides, giving a panoramic view. Isobel trailed her fingers along the bookcases on the front wall and met Greg's eyes when he followed her up the stairs.

"It's beautiful."

She wanted to say more—to ask how he could possibly afford such a house, to say something about this being the perfect reading room, to exclaim over the built-in bench cupboards in the corners—but she didn't know where to start.

His mouth crooked in a smile, as though he knew what she was thinking, and he walked over to her and caught her hands. "I thought you'd like it." He dropped a kiss on her forehead. "It's not actually on the market yet—the lawyer who's handling things for the owners had a heart attack, which delayed things."

"Oh, no. Is he okay?"

"She's doing much better. Her secretary says she should be back at work full time next week."

"And you wanted to make an offer before the house gets formally listed."

"Wouldn't you? I don't want to get into a bidding war on it."

She nodded. "I'm surprised you didn't make an offer already."

"I was tempted. The secretary was showing me around last night, and I really thought about making an offer on the spot, but I wanted to make sure you loved it as much as I do." He didn't give her a chance to answer him, instead stepping back and tugging on her hands. "Come on, you have to see the bedrooms."

Isobel followed him down the stairs, looking out the windows placed along the way. He wanted her to love the house. The closest he'd come to saying anything about a long-term commitment, though, was his comment at breakfast the other day about not running off. She pushed her worries to the back of her mind. They were together, and here, right now. Worrying about the future would only spoil today.

The bedrooms were up the main staircase. The first door on the right opened into a bathroom. Beyond, two bedrooms faced each other across the hall.

"Door at the end is a linen closet," Greg said. He opened the door to his immediate left. "Master bedroom."

It was huge, taking up two-thirds of the width of the house. Dormer windows looked out over the front and side with window seats nestled under them; toward the rear of the house was a walk-in closet and the master bath. The hardwood flooring continued in here, and all the trim matched. Isobel whistled.

"It's pretty much my dream house," Greg confessed. "The biggest knock against it at the moment is that a murder happened right across the street."

"Be sure to mention that during negotiations. Might keep the price down."

"I'll do that."

She sat down on one of the window seats and stared across the lawn. The trees screened the street, although come winter, he'd have a lovely view of both the minigolf course and the used car lot. "I wish we knew who did it. How safe will you feel here if the killer's still running loose?"

"Are you trying to talk me out of this place?" He sat at an angle, facing her but not looking out the window.

"Of course not. I just…" She shook her head. "I don't know. I'm sorry."

"What did you find out yesterday? I meant to call you back last night when I got in, but I pretty much crashed as soon as I got in the door."

"Nothing useful." She sighed. "Madge confirms the same putter was used on Father Paul and Richard. Sadie's going to give her petition to Michael so he can see whether there are any possible suspects who signed it. I still think Father Paul was just in the wrong place at the wrong time." She rubbed the blue fabric of the window seat absently. "Oh, and my boss may have been heartbroken about getting dumped, but I think her ex wants her back."

"And she's still grouchy?"

"Even more so, since I found that out by snooping in her office."

He laughed out loud. "Last year, I was the one who snooped in my boss's office."

"Yeah, but you didn't get caught."

"What'd she say?" He hesitated. "Is she going to be even more upset at you for leaving early today?"

She shrugged. "I told her I was looking for anything related to Enzian. She wasn't happy, and I can't blame her." She bit her lip. "But I found out just how unhappy I've been with all the extra stress she's put on me lately. I threatened to leave."

He didn't answer immediately, and when he did, his voice was low. "You told me you wouldn't leave."

Her chest tightened. She'd been worried about what his long-term thoughts were, and here she was, telling him that she might not stick around? That wasn't what she had meant.

"Greg—"

"At least you're telling me." He stood up. "Did you want to look at the rest of the place? I haven't been up to the attic yet."

She didn't move. "It was an empty threat. I feel overworked and unappreciated, but who doesn't?" She tried to make a joke of it. "Can you imagine what Momma would say if I told her I was moving, especially before Thanksgiving?"

He didn't smile. "Yes, I can."

He turned away. "If you need me, the trapdoor to the attic is in the rear bedroom."

"Greg!" She jumped up and grabbed at his arm. "I'm not leaving. Even if I left my job—which I have no intention of doing—I'd find another one in River Corners. This is my home. I'm not going anywhere." She paused, and when she spoke again, she was really quiet. "I can't leave you. I love you."

Momma had always said the woman shouldn't say it first. Momma said a lot of things. It didn't matter. Right now, Isobel knew she had hurt Greg, and she had to make it right.

"Please. Believe me. I'm not going anywhere."

He spoke without turning around to look at her. "You've told me about your father before, about how abandoned you felt when he left, about how your mother vowed never to trust another man. You said you were nothing like him."

"I'm not!"

"And you're right." He ignored her words. "You're your mother's daughter, afraid of commitment, afraid to trust, willing to do anything to avoid getting hurt."

"No…"

But hadn't Michael said the same thing many times? That she didn't even date because she was afraid of being left? She'd always said she was just waiting for the right guy. She'd found him—and now she might have scared him away.

"I think you need to have a long talk with your boss, without empty threats." The light glinted off his glasses as he finally turned to look at her, and she couldn't decide what his expression meant. "Let's go look at the attic."

CHAPTER TWENTY-SEVEN

Tuesday, June 22, late afternoon

For the rest of the house tour, Isobel felt like she was walking on eggshells. Afraid of Greg's reaction, she couldn't even figure out how to ask him why he thought her talking to Gerri would solve anything. Greg didn't make any more references to her leaving, but neither did they have their usual easy camaraderie.

While Greg locked up the front door once more, Isobel watched forlornly. She decided to try a joke. "At least we didn't come across any more bodies."

His lips twitched. "I'm sure Michael will be duly grateful."

"Before you take me home, could we make one more stop?" Her words rushed out. "We are in the neighborhood, after all, and we agreed that we needed to poke around the car dealership to see if anyone saw anything, and there won't be a lot of other customers there right now. You can test drive the convertible, too," she trailed off.

"We might as well."

He led the way to the car, stopping to hold her door open for her. The drive wasn't wide enough here to turn around, and he went around the house to the garage, which had a turn-around area cleared next to it.

Isobel stared wistfully up at the tower room, its windows clearly visible from here. She did love the house.

In fact, there were no other customers at the car lot, only Jim Butler and one salesman.

"Hey, folks!" Jim greeted them as they got out of the car again. "You looking to trade in?"

"I might be willing to trade in my car," Isobel said. "Both Greg and my cousin keep giving me grief about my current one. I wanted to see what you have first."

His smile faded a notch as he realized he wouldn't be making a sale today. He quickly recovered, however. "Certainly, certainly! What kind of car are you looking for? A coupe? Family sedan? Minivan?"

Isobel's face twisted. Why in the world would anyone think she wanted a mom-mobile? It was fine for Kimberley, who used her van for work-related activities, including bringing home loads of plants and flowers to prep for events, but Isobel didn't need anything that big.

"I was thinking something small and cozy," she said.

"Could we look at that sweet little convertible up front?" Greg asked.

Jim smiled knowingly. "That one draws them all in. You wouldn't like to take it for a test drive, would you?"

"Well, maybe."

Isobel snorted. "I'll just poke around the lot, see what else you have, if that's all right?"

"Sure, sure," Jim said, leading Greg away. "It's an older model, that's true, but the previous owner had it converted to run on unleaded gasoline, so that won't be any problem. She handles like a dream. You can drive a stick, right? You just have to be careful or you'll look down and find yourself going over eighty without even thinking about it."

Shaking her head, Isobel walked over to the more conservative imports. The salesman trailed her.

"Are you looking for a two- or four-door model?" he asked her. "In the long run, the four-door is the better deal, whether you're using the back seat for people or groceries. It's just easier to get in and out." He led her over to a Corolla. "Last winter, my aunt fell on the ice and broke her ankle, and let me tell you, it was quite a chore trying to get her in and out of my dad's two-door."

"I imagine it would be," Isobel murmured.

These cars weren't all that different from the one she already owned, and there wouldn't really be much point in getting a newer car of the same type. On the other hand, she didn't think there was much point anyway. She was here to get clues—and to let Greg test drive the convertible, in an admittedly weak attempt to strengthen their relationship.

In retrospect, it was a good thing she hadn't been able to reach him on the phone the night before. That conversation would have been even more disastrous on the phone. Why had she said that to Gerri in the first place? She knew why she'd told Greg—it would never have occurred to her not to.

She paused at one car painted with pink and green stripes. Bumper stickers for every tourist attraction in driving distance plastered the back of the car, obviously predating the current magnetic sticker wave. "What were they thinking?"

The salesman shrugged. "I don't ask. I just let them know what we can offer on the car as a trade-in."

"I don't imagine they got much on this."

His face pinched together, and he didn't answer. Probably thought she wouldn't offer much for it if she knew what they'd paid—not that she had any intention of offering anything anyway.

"That was a four, not a three!" An angry voice carried from the minigolf course, and they looked over, then back at the car in front of them.

"You see a lot of what goes on over there?" Isobel asked.

"I wasn't working the day of the murder." His voice was bored, like he'd answered the same question a dozen times already. "So no, I didn't see anything."

"But you see things other days, don't you? Like the kids who sneak in because they don't want to pay?"

"Oh, those." He sniffed. "Yes, a couple times a week I have to chase out the teenagers who want to use our lot as a shortcut. I'm happy to see them go over there, though—otherwise, they try to use our vehicles for making out. This one time, I was showing minivans to a mother with her two kids, and when I opened the hatchback—well, I managed to get it closed before the kids got an eyeful, anyway."

"Oh my." Isobel blinked. "But aren't the cars kept locked?"

"Only at night," he told her. "During the day, customers have to be able to wander around, look inside, see how it feels to sit in the driver's seat." He held open a door to a Corolla for her. "Take this one, for instance. The former owners had the seats custom upholstered in microsuede. You've never sat on such a comfortable seat."

The tan seats *did* look soft. Isobel ran her hand along the seat back, then sat down. "Very comfortable." She wiggled against the seat. "Almost too comfortable. I'd be afraid of falling asleep at the wheel."

If the salesman wasn't working the day of the murder, he wouldn't have any idea who might have sneaked in that afternoon. Isobel racked her brain, trying to come up with another way to get the information she wanted. She hoped Greg was getting something useful from Butler, other than the mileage of the convertible.

"It's not that bad, really," the salesman said. "You can take it for a test drive and see for yourself. I borrowed it last week to take my girlfriend's mother over to Weston, and neither one of us fell asleep. Too bad," he added. "I could have used a break from her nagging."

Isobel stared up at him. "You can borrow the cars from the lot?"

"Oh, sure. It's one of the perks of working here. Jim lets everyone borrow the cars—salesmen, the secretary, his wife." He nodded toward the front of the lot. "That convertible's gotten a lot of mileage since it got traded in, let me tell you."

"Maybe I should moonlight here instead of trading in my car," she joked.

"Jim's not hiring right now."

"I was kidding. I've got more to do than time to do it in, anyway." She grabbed the door frame to help herself out of the car. "I was just thinking that then I could use different cars for different occasions. Maybe get a pickup truck the next time I get a Christmas tree." She sighed. He wouldn't understand the reference. "I don't suppose Jim does car rentals?"

"I don't think anyone's ever asked him before." He closed the door firmly. "No test drive, then? Maybe I could interest you in something a little sportier, like a Jeep? Or we have half a dozen minivans. You might not want one now, but when the kids come along..."

Kids. She tensed; she was totally not prepared to think about that. She glanced toward the front of the lot; there was no way Greg had heard the comment. She relaxed her shoulders. Although a little boy with hair like his—no, this was not the time for daydreaming.

"I'll bet none of you ever borrow the minivans," she said dryly.

"You wouldn't think so, but one got signed out this weekend." He pointed to a dark red van with a metallic finish. "Came back all cleaned and polished, vacuumed and everything."

She walked toward the minivan. There was something about what he'd said, but she couldn't put her finger on it. "You don't usually give them back clean?"

He snorted. "Bob and I have to wash them all down once a week so they show nice. Besides, we'd just cleaned them Friday—we were supposed to do it Saturday, but Bob had a date Friday night, so he wanted to do it early."

The minivan was cleaned on Friday, then cleaned again on Saturday. That had to be important. She reached out to open the back gate. It wouldn't open.

"I thought you said they were kept unlocked."

"It should be." He opened the driver's door and hit a switch. The car dinged and the gate started to come up. She caught a glimpse of the gray carpet interior and dark splotches that might be shadows or stains.

Then a hand reached past her and pushed the gate back down. Jim Butler's voice said jovially, "You don't need to look at these. You're young yet; you have time before you get tied down."

"But—"

He was the one who had suggested she look at minivans in the first place. She glanced past him, but Greg wasn't there to back her up. Even if he were, he might mistake the reason she wanted to look. Why did they have to get into a fight today?

"Your boyfriend's taking the convertible for a spin. Why don't we see what else you might fit into?" Jim put his arm around her shoulders and pulled her away from the minivan.

"Oh, I wasn't looking at the minivan for me," she babbled. "My friend Kimberley said she was thinking about changing out her old one. Wants something newer, with more flexibility in the back, you know?"

"I'll be happy to show her the minivans if she comes in." He didn't relax his arm. "Why don't you come look at these sedans? A little bigger than the compacts Freddy was showing you, with lots more features."

He obviously wasn't going to let her poke around on her own, even though he knew she wasn't going to be buying today. He must have something to hide, and it was probably related to that red minivan.

She had no one to tell. Greg was off with the convertible, probably enjoying himself without her, and Michael—well, she could probably call him, but she wasn't even sure what she could tell him, let alone how to do so with Jim still holding on to her.

Resigned, she let Jim steer her toward the sedans. It was daylight, the other salesman—Freddy—knew she was there, and Greg would be back at any minute. Nothing would happen to her. She hoped.

"Freddy, why don't you go take care of your paperwork? Get it done, and you can go home early."

He'd just gotten rid of the only witness. Now she worried.

CHAPTER TWENTY-EIGHT

Tuesday, June 22, late afternoon

"I'm not really interested in sedans," Isobel said, doing her best to hang back despite Butler pulling her along.

She hadn't done anything suspicious, had she? She was just talking to the salesman.

"Sedans have changed. We're not talking full-size cars like the old Cadillac gunboats," he said. "Just comfy, with more room to stretch out."

"I'd really rather just go wait for Greg to get back. I think I've seen enough for one day." She hadn't really seen anything in the minivan—maybe enough for Michael to come check it out, although he'd be mad that she'd been looking around. Why was Butler being so insistent?

"I'm sure Greg would want you to do your own little test drive." He paused next to a dark gray Ford that didn't look that different from the compacts she had been looking at, except for being bigger.

"Maybe."

He had to have done it. Why else steer her away from the minivan—the car that had been taken out and cleaned the day Richard had been attacked? It didn't make sense, though. Richard had been attacked in the cupboard, hadn't he? There hadn't been marks in the garage for him being dragged around. So what would be in the car?

It didn't make sense.

She had to keep him talking, keep him busy until Greg got back. Even if Butler knew she suspected something, he wouldn't do anything rash. She shook her head mentally. More rash than killing Father Paul and assaulting Richard? This was a man who thrived on taking chances.

"Freddy was telling me you sometimes have problems with teens using your cars for things they shouldn't."

He grunted. "No one's been in this car. You want me to get the portable blacklight to prove it?"

"You keep one of those on hand?"

"When we get a trade-in, we have to clean it up real good. Get out all the grease and salt from spilled fast food, get rid of the traces of blood from mother's little angel whose nose bled all over the back seat, and make sure there's nothing else a buyer's going to object to. It's a little more work, but our customers appreciate it."

That made sense. Of course, it also made her wonder what kind of stains the back of the minivan might hold after he'd already cleaned it. Not blood—he'd already said he knew how to clean that up.

Butler finally dropped his arm from around her shoulders and opened the doors of the sedan. "Look at how much room you have in here. Even your friend Greg would have plenty of legroom."

She peered in. Yes, both Greg and Michael would be able to stretch their legs out in the backseat. She tried to remember the last time her cousin had ridden anywhere with her. Probably when he'd been teaching her to drive. So, not an issue.

"Jim, I'm all done," Freddy called from the small glassed-in building on the back of the lot. "See you tomorrow?"

"Yeah." Butler gave him a casual wave. "You left your paperwork on top of my desk?"

"No, I stuck it in that new cupboard—you know, the one that looks like you took it out of your garage."

"All right, I'll find it." Butler turned back to face Isobel, but she wasn't listening.

Garage cupboards…she was willing to bet that Jim Butler lived in the new subdivision and that if Michael went over to Butler's house right now, there would be a gap in the cupboards. She could see it now—Richard had probably gone over to ask him to tone down the negativity in the ads, and instead Butler had killed him and stuffed him into a cupboard. Then he took the cupboard and moved it to an empty house down the block, taking out a cupboard of the same size. That explained the sawdust Madge had mentioned.

Why hadn't he put the clean cupboard back in his garage? Because he had to come to work, and the cupboard was in the van—so he took the cupboard out and stored it in his office. The stains in the back were probably grease from bolts or something of the sort. Or maybe they weren't stains at all, but tears in the carpet. It all made sense, except—

"Why Father Paul?"

He acted as if he hadn't heard her, walking around to the back of the car. "Let me show you the trunk."

Isobel shook her head. "Why Father Paul? I can almost see why you'd attack Richard—you probably didn't think you could win the election—but why?"

"You'd be amazed what you can fit back here. Come look at the subwoofers in here. We could take them out if you want, for a fee, of course."

Confused, Isobel stepped closer. He had heard her, hadn't he? But he was still talking as if she were going to buy the car.

She just had time to notice that there were, in fact, four speakers in the trunk of the car before he grabbed her and shoved her inside. The lid slammed shut.

There was room—barely—for her inside the trunk, but not enough room to move around. She might be able to hit the trunk lid, but she couldn't get any force behind it. With the subwoofer in the way, she couldn't even feel for a latch to open the back seat from here. Assuming any cars still had that feature.

Car doors slammed, and the engine started. And she hadn't thought this could get any worse.

The sound system turned on. Great—now no one would even be able to hear her yell for help.

Butler had to be desperate. When Greg got back, he'd wonder where she was—wait! She could call him. Or Michael. Maybe both.

She reached for her phone and realized it was in her messenger bag, still in Greg's car. Another clue for him that she hadn't just wandered off. She hoped he got back soon.

The car started to move.

No! Butler was taking her somewhere else to kill her. There'd be clues here, but he didn't care. Or had he grabbed her bag from Greg's car? She couldn't remember whether Greg had locked the car.

If she got out of this, she would convince Greg, somehow, that she had no intention of leaving. That he was all she wanted.

She teared up. No—she would not be some helpless damsel. She got into this on her own, and she could get out of it. She rubbed her eyes with the back of her hand and took a deep breath. It was hard to think, lying on the speakers with the music pounding into her skull.

Exhaling, she peered at the trunk, but she couldn't see any light. Whoever had installed the speakers had evidently sealed the trunk up tight so road noise wouldn't interfere with the sound. She'd have to explore by touch.

The cramped space made checking out the compartment difficult, but she forced herself through pain and discomfort. She wasn't about to be Butler's next victim.

She felt some wires and cables with her right hand; one of them might be the trunk release. She started pulling. One of the speakers crackled and died. Isobel bit her lip. She didn't want to disconnect the speakers entirely—Butler would figure she was up to something and might act sooner.

Her fingers ran over the strands again, and she closed her eyes to concentrate—not that it changed what she saw, but it gave her the illusion of control. There, that one stabbed, a sharp metal wire frayed off a braided metal cable. That was the one she wanted. She tugged on it.

Nothing happened.

Maybe she'd pulled it the wrong way? She should trace the path of the cable, see if that helped, although the wire was scraping her palm. Isobel shifted to bring her left hand up, and she felt a lever.

Oh. How simple.

Squirming, she repositioned herself, bringing her right arm up to grab at a strut on the trunk lid. It wouldn't do for the lid to fling up suddenly.

The shift in position made her realize her legs were beginning to cramp. If they went to sleep, she'd be lucky to be able to climb out of the car, let alone run away. She flexed her muscles and wiggled her toes. Keep the circulation going.

She took another deep breath and exhaled, then pulled on the lever. The lid opened an inch. A gust of air blew into the opening, threatening to push the lid all the way up. Her right arm strained to keep it down, low enough to see out but hopefully not high enough to catch Butler's attention.

Butler was driving through downtown!

The Miniature Golf Course Murders

The tents for Summerfest fluttered white off to her left, and the familiar buildings of the college stood along the left. She'd expected Butler to take her somewhere desolate to kill her, but maybe he was heading back to the subdivision. It didn't matter. She knew where she was, and her chance to escape was coming up.

Butler reached a stop sign and tapped his brakes.

Isobel flung the trunk lid open and scrambled for the edge. Her legs didn't want to move well, despite her efforts to keep them awake, and she wound up tumbling onto the ground rather than landing gracefully. She crawled along the ground, dragging herself for a sidewalk. Please, please, don't let him put the car in reverse!

"Isobel?" Sadie's voice. "What are you doing in the street?"

Butler floored the car, taking off through the intersection amid a flurry of honks and yells. It didn't matter. Michael would get him.

Right now, Isobel accepted Sadie's helping hand to the sidewalk, where she collapsed, stretching her legs out in front of her. "Can I borrow your cellphone?"

CHAPTER TWENTY-NINE

Tuesday, June 22, end of the day

Explaining to Michael wasn't easy. She was still on the phone, trying to convince him to go after Butler when Greg pulled up alongside the sidewalk and stopped, even though it was a no-parking zone. He took the phone from her unceremoniously.

"Your cousin was kidnapped, and you're yelling at her instead of going after the guy? Are you crazy?"

He listened to what Michael had to say, then hung up and handed the phone back to Isobel, who returned it to Sadie.

"Kidnapped?" Sadie had been quiet through the phone call.

"Yes, kidnapped." Isobel pushed her hair out of her face. Hadn't she said that at some point while talking to Michael? She was sure she had, but maybe not. "You know many other reasons people crawl out of the trunks of moving vehicles?"

"Did you really?" Greg sat on the sidewalk next to her and wrapped his arms around her. "I should take you over to the clinic to get checked out."

"In a little bit." She snuggled against him. She started to shake. That had been a closer call than last year. Maybe she should be taking self-defense lessons instead of cooking classes. "I did wait until he stopped at the stop sign."

She looked up at Sadie. "Thank you for the phone."

"Kidnapped?" Sadie asked again. "Who did it?"

"Jim Butler." She shook her head. "I still don't know why…"

Isobel let her voice trail off. Let Sadie think she was talking about why Butler had kidnapped her. Right now, Isobel didn't have the emotional reserves to cope with the other woman's reaction. She glanced up at Sadie again. "Could you, possibly, go over to the diner for me? I could use something hot and sweet to drink." She held up one hand to show her continuing shakiness. "Please?"

Sadie nodded. "I'll be right back."

Instead of watching her go, Isobel leaned in against Greg and closed her eyes. "I was so afraid—"

"Shhh." He stroked her hair. "You're safe now."

"I know, but—" She swallowed. "I was afraid I wouldn't see you, wouldn't get the chance to tell you I'm so sorry. You know I don't want to leave you, right?"

He pulled her onto his lap. "Good. I don't want you to."

They sat like that, waiting for Sadie to come back. When she got there, she handed each of them a paper cup with hot coffee. "I hope it's sweet enough. I've never had to do this before."

Isobel took a sip and grimaced. "Yes, that's sweet enough."

Sweet enough to power an entire neighborhood of hyperactive kids, but she didn't say that. She sipped at the coffee again. "Thank you."

Fifteen minutes later, a police car pulled up, and the driver got out and walked around the front of the car. "Sir, you're blocking traffic. If you don't move, I'm going to have to give you a ticket."

Greg opened his mouth to say something, but Isobel cut him off. "Has my cousin picked up Butler yet?"

The policeman blinked, nonplussed. "Excuse me?"

"My cousin Michael? Your boss, the police chief? Has he arrested Butler for kidnapping me yet?"

"Oh, you're the one!" The policeman toggled the radio on his shoulder. "Dispatch, this is Hunt. I've found her. Corner of Third and Main. Some minor lacerations, no major injuries visible."

"Bring her in. Chief's on his way back, and he wants to talk to her."

"Ten-four." Officer Hunt looked down at Greg and Isobel. "Chief's driving the whole department crazy looking for you."

"What about Butler?" Isobel brushed aside Michael's concern.

"Chief called the judge and warrants were on his desk in something like five minutes flat. He drove to Butler's house himself, and sent a team to the car lot to gather evidence." He gestured for them to stand up. "If you don't mind, you do still need to move your car—and I'm supposed to take you in to the station."

"Greg will drive me over," Isobel said. "You can escort us, if you insist."

Greg frowned, but stood, then reached down to help her up. She winced at the pressure on her hands and blew on the palms after he let go.

He frowned and looked at them. "You should get those looked at."

"At the station." She shook her hands lightly. "Madge may want to look at them."

He frowned but didn't argue.

Isobel turned to Sadie. "Thanks again for the use of your phone. I'm sorry about the blood on it."

Under ordinary circumstances, Isobel would have walked to the police station, but she still felt shaky—and she wanted to stay near Greg. He held the door for her, then buckled her in and dropped a kiss on her forehead before closing the door.

Hunt motioned for them to park in one of the reserved spots in front of the station, and he slid a green plastic card under their windshield wiper. Then he led them into the station.

As the door opened, Momma's voice carried over the sound of others talking. "—should be your first priority. Don't make me talk to your mothers."

Isobel balked. She wasn't ready to run into Momma.

Greg eased her forward. "It'll be all right," he whispered. "She loves you. We all do."

She looked up at him. Had she heard him right? It wasn't the most romantic place for him to say he loved her, but then again, she'd said it in the middle of a fight in an empty house.

Then she didn't have time to think about it any more—Momma had seen her.

"Isobel! Are you all right? These people can't seem to tell me anything!"

"I'll be fine, Momma. What are you doing here?"

"A fine question! I hear my daughter—my only child—has escaped from a crazed murderer—and you think I would be somewhere else?"

Isobel let her momma fold her into a hug before drawing back and saying, "I think Michael needs to talk to me about what happened, and they probably have paperwork I have to do. Greg can bring me by when I'm done."

"You think I can just go and leave you here?"

"Greg's with me. And you know Michael won't do anything that would get you or Aunt Rosa angry at him."

"He'd better not!"

Isobel leaned in and kissed her momma on the cheek. "I'll be fine. Go home. Cook. Bake. Summerfest starts Friday, you know."

"You come home just as soon as you can." Momma shook her finger at Isobel, nodded at Greg, and swept from the station.

Moments later, Michael strode in, his face thunderous, and Isobel shook. Maybe she'd sent Momma home too soon; Isobel could use the buffer against her cousin.

"My office. Now," he barked. "Stone can wait out here."

Isobel squared her shoulders. "No."

"Excuse me?" His voice was quiet, and all of the police officers busied themselves looking at anything but him.

"No," she repeated. "I'm not going into your office alone so you can bully, badger, and browbeat me. If I'm going in, he's coming with me." Stinging in her hands reminded her of her shredded skin, and she lifted her palms for his inspection. "Oh, and can we do something about these?"

His eyebrows lowered even more, but he didn't say anything to her. He glanced at the desk officer. "Tell Madge to come to my office and bring both an evidence kit and a first aid kit."

This time, when he jerked his head at his office, Isobel followed, grateful for Greg's arm around her shoulders.

Michael waited only until the office door closed behind her. "What the hell do you think you were doing?"

"I was looking at used cars."

"By yourself?" He rounded on Greg. "Where were you when she was grabbed and stuffed into a trunk?"

"You leave him—" Isobel started, but Greg interrupted.

"No, he's right. I went off joyriding in the convertible and left you alone on the lot. We didn't know the murderer owned it, but we *did* know that Father Paul's murder had happened right next door. There's no excuse."

Consequences hadn't been at the forefront of their minds; their fight had. It had colored everything. But she was damned if she was going to give her cousin the satisfaction of hearing about that.

Isobel thrust her chin out at Michael. "So if I'd called you and said I was going to go look at cars, you would have sent an officer with me to keep me out of trouble?"

He wouldn't have; they both knew it. There was no reason to suspect Butler of anything except bad taste in commercials. He glowered at her anyway and opened his mouth to say something when a knock came at the door.

A moment later, Madge stepped inside and set two kits down on Michael's desk. She tsked over Isobel's hands while working with tweezers to lift minuscule wires and place them into labeled evidence baggies. "Sorry. I know I'm making it worse. This should have been done as soon as possible." She shot a glance at Michael before cleaning Isobel's palms and fingers with an antiseptic pad. "You're going to want to go easy on these for a few days. Keep ointment on them, and keep them wrapped up. Less scarring that way."

"Thank you," Isobel gasped. Why did rubbing alcohol sting so much? "I didn't realize there were bits of wire in there."

Madge shrugged as she squeezed ointment onto Isobel's hands. "I already got bloody wire samples from the car trunk, so it seemed a safe bet." She grinned fiercely. "And now we have an airtight evidence trail; it's not just your word against his."

That hadn't even occurred to Isobel. She felt faint.

"Do you think this will go to trial?" Greg asked.

"Too soon to tell," Michael said. "A smart lawyer would tell him to plea bargain, but Butler strikes me as the type to fight every step of the way."

Isobel nodded. "So he didn't confess to anything?"

"Clammed right up, said he was invoking his Fifth Amendment rights, and said nothing more."

"We'll never know why he killed Father Paul?"

"No, I got a statement from Richard finally. I called him when your call came in. Told him that his silence had almost gotten you killed. Some of it—specifically about Father Paul—is hearsay and inadmissible, but it gives us the background anyway."

"Why? I asked him—" Too late, she realized that she'd admitted to knowing she might be in danger, but she plowed on anyway. "After I saw the minivan and Freddy made the comments about the cupboard, I knew he had to have done it. I asked him why, and he didn't say anything, just shoved me into the trunk."

"You knew and you stayed there?" Michael had started calming down, but now he was livid again.

"What, I was going to walk alone down Main Street? Or try to barricade myself in Greg's car and hope that Butler didn't have a matching key? I was just hoping to keep him talking until Greg got back."

"That worked well, didn't it? Isobel, when are you going to learn?" He stood up, towering over her. "It's not safe for you to poke your nose into these things."

She tried to clench her hands into fists, but Madge was still swaddling them in bandages, and Isobel found she could barely flex her fingers. "Yes, and you were going to solve it any time now, weren't you?"

Silence fell in the office, and Isobel realized she'd gone too far. She bit her lip.

"I'm sorry," she said quietly.

Michael moved around behind his desk and sat down. "According to Richard, Father Paul was just in the wrong place at the wrong time. Butler had planned to frame Richard for the murder—showed up at the Holsteins' house to leave the bloody putter in Richard's car. Richard surprised him. He doesn't remember much but confused impressions between that and waking up in the hospital; the doctors say that's natural with the battering his head took."

"Butler's lawyer will probably say Richard's evidence is suspect because of the head trauma. Try to get it all thrown out," Madge said. "Fortunately, we have a whiz with evidence, if I do say so myself. I'll be able to place Butler in Holstein's garage—and probably Holstein in Butler's garage, where Butler shoved him into the cupboard and hit him more. We'll be able to prove it."

"All's well that ends well, then." Isobel leaned back in her chair and stared at her hands, which had been wrapped up like the Invisible Man's. "I'll have to tell Kimberley I can't help her any more with Summerfest, though."

"I'm sure she'll manage." Michael wasn't ready to forgive her yet. "Believe it or not, most of us can do our jobs without you butting in."

Silently, Isobel counted to six. He was upset because he was worried. As Greg had said, they all loved her. Instead of yelling at him about this not being the time, she changed the subject. "Did you want to bring in an officer for me to give a statement to? Momma asked me to come over as soon as I could. I rather think she wanted me to leave the station with her."

As she'd hoped, the mention of her mother got his attention.

"I'll send someone in to take your statement." He glanced at her hands. "I'll expect you to come back and sign it next week."

Next week? Gerri was going to hate her being out of commission that long. On the other hand, it did mean she wouldn't have to deal with Enzian again right now. Maybe she could put that off until the ghostwriter sent the finished copy back.

Michael stood. "Don't think this lets you off the hook. We will talk about this later."

She was sure they would.

CHAPTER THIRTY

Saturday, June 26

"I knew I should have sneaked some of Momma's cookies. The line for her booth never ends," Isobel said gloomily.

Summerfest had started, and the town square was packed with white tents, booths with no tents, and crowds of people jostling to see and do everything. Father Terrence had even done a reasonable job with the opening prayer, although as Aunt Rosa said, he'd never be another Father Paul.

"You wouldn't want to disappoint her adoring fans, would you?" Greg asked.

"I don't want to disappoint *me*."

He chuckled. "What if I were to tell you I convinced her to sell me some in advance?"

She stopped walking and stared at him. "How in the world did you do that?"

"Believe it or not, she adores you," he said. "She was happy to do it, as long as it doesn't compromise her dream—and if you'd offered her money, she would've been insulted."

"But she could take it from you. That makes sense, in a weird, twisted, Momma sort of way." She shook her head and resumed walking. "What do you want to do first? My only request is that we stay away from the games area."

"I always thought that was half the fun of these events."

"Usually. On the other hand, they always have a couple putting holes for the kids, and right now, the last thing I want to see is another golf putter."

"One advantage of being tall—I'll see them first and make sure to steer you away," he said. "But I've always liked the game where you throw darts at balloons."

"They underinflate the balloons, you know."

"It's still fun."

Together, they wended through the crowd away from the food booths. Isobel nodded to familiar faces, people she'd known since childhood, vendors she'd collected fees from the other day for Kimberley, even Michael and Violet. Her cousin narrowed his eyes at her, and she gave him back an innocent blink. She *hadn't* known what would happen at the car lot, and he'd had several days to cool down, but he was obviously still miffed at her.

"What are you two up to?" Violet called.

"He wants to go break some balloons."

Michael frowned. "You know they're underinflated, right?"

Greg looked from Michael to Isobel. "So I've been told. Do you two want to spoil everyone's fun?"

Isobel met Michael's eyes, and they both laughed. "I won't tell if you won't tell."

Michael shook his head. "There's a reason you were never asked to staff a booth again."

"No one could prove anything." Isobel sulked. "Besides, everyone had fun! And I didn't get hit by nearly as many falling darts."

Greg glanced at her sidelong. "How old were you at the time?"

Isobel looked everywhere but at him. "If you two were planning on picking up some of Momma's cookies, it's going to be a long wait. I think there were more people in line at her booth than the rest of the food vendors combined."

Her cousin held up a plain white baker's bag and let it swing back and forth.

"Did she give everybody cookies before me?"

Violet said, "She said you already had yours."

Isobel glowered up at Greg. "Well, one of us does."

Michael popped open the bag and plucked out a lemon cookie. "Mmmm."

"I hope you brought enough to share," drawled a familiar voice.

Isobel whirled. "Dante!"

She threw her arms around him. He winced, and she drew back carefully. He was thinner, but his color was good. "Sorry. I'm just so happy to see you. How are you doing?"

"Better. Much better." He squeezed her arms. "I'm in remission. My oncologist isn't convinced it's going to last, but I plan to enjoy it while it lasts. So what's this I hear from your momma about you solving another murder?"

The sound of Michael grinding his teeth behind her was surely her imagination. Isobel didn't check, though. "It was a fluke. I was in the right place at the wrong time, and things just clicked."

She wanted to drop the subject; she didn't think Michael would ever completely stop talking to her, but there was no reason to push it.

Greg reached past Isobel to shake Dante's hand. "Are you staying in town?"

"I'm moving back, yes." He flashed his familiar grin. "You might have competition for Isobel again. In fact, I was planning to ask her to move in with me."

Michael tried to pretend his laugh was a cough. Violet giggled. Isobel ignored them, cocking her head to one side.

"Explain?"

"My mother's idea, of course. I'm sure she thinks if we're living together, we'll both change our minds and live happily ever after, but she didn't say so."

"What did she say, then?" Isobel asked.

"That it would be a good idea for me to not be on my own in case I have a relapse. I have to admit it, it does sound reasonable." His eyes flicked from her to Greg and back, and he waggled his eyebrows. "If you have other commitments, though, I'll understand."

Heat flooded her face. At least Dante hadn't said this in front of her momma, although saying it in front of Michael was bad enough. She risked a glance at Greg, who winked at her. Worse and worse. She didn't need to think about his lovely new home with all the built-in bookshelves and the bathtub big enough for two.

"Is this your surprise?" Isobel frowned at Dante. "Kimberley did tell me she's planning to put the house on the market, so I will need someplace to live. I hadn't planned to worry about it until the issue came up, though."

He patted her shoulder. "That's my girl. Always thinking ahead."

"I did have other things on my mind, you know."

Greg slid his arm around her shoulders, and she leaned into him gratefully. He said, "I think it's a great idea—for now." Isobel's heart sped up at the implicit promise of those last two words, but she didn't say anything and Greg continued, "And it'll give you someone else to practice your cooking skills on."

Dante blanched.

Isobel didn't bother telling him that she'd gotten better, thanks to Momma's cooking lessons. She could invite him for Thanksgiving dinner, and he'd see for himself. Instead, she said, "But you sublet the Blue Iguana. What will you do with yourself?"

Shrugging, Dante said, "I'll get by. I invested a good chunk of my profits, and I've still got some of the investments, even after medical expenses." Looking over Isobel's head, he said, "You never did say whether you had enough cookies to share."

"I'd be happy to give you one," Michael said. "Isobel's on her own, though."

Violet passed the bag to Dante, who took a cookie, then held it out to both Greg and Isobel.

"Nobody takes me seriously around here." Michael looked into the bag mournfully before taking another cookie. "They're already a quarter gone. I'm going to need to buy more."

"Good idea." Isobel shifted so she could see her cousin. "Better get in line now before she sells out."

"What are you up to this time?"

"Why do you always assume the worst?"

"Because I've known you your entire life."

His eyes were narrowed again, and Isobel knew if she said anything more, they were both going to regret this conversation. She opened her mouth anyway.

"Look at the time!" Dante interrupted. "We'd better all head over if we're going to be there for the big announcement."

"Head over where?" "What big announcement?"

Dante didn't answer, however, simply turning and striding off into the crowd. Isobel looked up at Greg, shrugged, and followed. To her surprise, he stopped about ten feet from Momma's booth.

Momma glanced over at them and nodded, then raised her hands to get people's attention. A voice came from the line. "Oh, no! She's sold out." Murmurs passed back through the line.

"I am *not* sold out." Momma didn't yell. She didn't need to; everyone heard her. The muttering faded. "I have plenty of cookies and will be selling for the entire run of Summerfest." Scattered applause and a few cheers. She waited for silence. "I will also be opening a bakery after Summerfest is over. Dante has agreed to sublet me his shop, and next week, Momma's Cookies will be opening in the former Blue Iguana."

Dante gave her a half bow. "My pleasure."

This time, the applause was sustained, and Momma broke it off by looking at the next person in line. "What would you like?"

Isobel stared at Dante. "*That* was your big surprise, wasn't it? Not that you were coming back. You...you conspired with Momma behind my back!"

"Guilty as charged." He grinned. "She did let me pick out the uniforms, though. She'll be hiring extra help to run the counter."

Sensible. Momma couldn't do it all on her own. She'd obviously been planning this for quite some time, to have all the permits and business licenses, to get the shop set up—and to talk to both Kimberley and Dante about what she was doing without letting Isobel know.

Isobel crossed her arms in front of her.

"Stings, doesn't it?" Michael patted her on the head, which he knew annoyed her. "You'd think people could talk to their family about important things like this."

She scowled up at him, even though it put her neck at an awkward angle. "She planned this."

"I'm supposed to feel better because you didn't plan to put yourself in danger? I warned you it was going to happen. Several times."

"You weren't interested in talking to me." She turned her back on the booth. "Come on, Greg, we have some balloons to throw darts at."

He walked beside her in silence. Finally, she said, "What was I supposed to do? When I did try talking to him, he wouldn't listen!"

"Did you see today's headline?"

Before she could answer him, Sue Holstein stepped in front of them, forcing them to stop. "Isobel. Thank you for finding the killer. You might be spoiled, but you did a good job. Unlike that police chief—I don't care if he is your cousin."

Isobel gave the other woman an icy glare. She and Michael might be at odds right now, but that didn't give anyone else the right to criticize him. "Michael could do his job much better if everyone cooperated. I understand Richard refused to say who attacked him. That would have solved the case right there."

Sue flushed. "He was afraid it would come across as a smear campaign against his opponent. Jim Butler was using every dirty trick in the book, but Richard's better than that."

"Right. Because not telling the truth is *such* a noble thing to do."

It didn't sound like Richard. Worrying that people might think he was smearing his opponent, maybe—but Isobel was willing to bet Sue had been behind the silence. She was the one who worried about what other people thought.

Isobel fixed Sue in the eye. "I'm glad Richard's recovering. I'm glad he's still going to be our mayor; I think he does a good job. But if you had the sense God gave a geranium, you would have used this time to get closer to people in the community instead of insulting everyone who tried to give you any help. Good-bye, Sue."

They had reached the first of the game booths—throw a pingpong ball into a goldfish bowl and win the fish—before Isobel spoke again. "I'm sorry. She just rubs me the wrong way. I'm not being a very fun date today."

Greg looped his arm around her shoulders and squeezed. "I think you were being too harsh on the geraniums, to be honest."

She laughed, slid her arm around his waist, and squeezed back. It was good to have someone who understood. "Come on, let's go find the balloons."

"You never did tell me how old you were when you manned the booth," he teased. "I could ask your mother."

They'd reached the balloon booth, which was being manned by Annie and Christy. "Three darts for a dollar. Pop a balloon, win a prize!"

Annie frowned at Isobel. "My grandmother said you're not supposed to be here. Your name's on a list."

"How many other names are on the list?" Greg asked.

"Just hers. Do you know three years ago, everyone walked away a winner?" Annie sounded scandalized.

"As opposed to all of the five years before, when no one won at all," Isobel defended herself. "How many prizes have you given out so far this year?"

"Two," said Christy.

"Then my crusade was not in vain."

"Three years?" Greg said. "Three years ago, you were rigging games?"

"I was volunteering. And I was only banned from volunteering for the game booths—not from playing them."

He chuckled and pulled out his wallet. "Give me five dollars' worth," he told the girls. "Don't worry—I won't let her throw them."

As if she could with her hands still encased in bandages.

Greg stubbornly refused to listen when Isobel pointed out the balloons he'd have the best chance of popping, but he still won two small bears. "His and hers," he said, giving one to Isobel and keeping one himself.

Isobel accepted her bear, admiring the red and pink hearts printed all over it. "You could have won a bigger prize, though."

"That's not the point. I'm having fun, they're earning money, life is good. You don't always have to win, Isobel."

She sighed. "You're talking about Michael again, aren't you? It's not my fault the newspaper said I should have his job!"

"You did see the article, then."

"It was on the front page. How could I miss it?" Especially with multiple copies casually left on her doorstep. "But he knows no one believes the paper!"

"He'll cool off. Just don't find any bodies for a while."

"No problem." She leaned against him. "I'm done with dead bodies."

"Famous last words."

Sara Penhallow is the mystery-writing pseudonym of Erin M. Hartshorn. She fell in love with the mystery genre when she first picked up an Encyclopedia Brown book; thereafter, she spent hours devouring everything from Nancy Drew and Trixie Belden to Agatha Christie, John Carr, Ed McBain, and Nancy Pickard. When she's not writing, she enjoys various handicrafts and spending time with her family. She blogs online at sarapenhallow.erinmhartshorn.com and can be found on Twitter (@SaraPenhallow).

And now a special bonus peek at the next River Corners Mystery,

THE CORN MAZE MURDERS

CHAPTER ONE

Saturday, November 13

Momma's Cookies, the downtown bakery named for (and run by) Isobel Santini's momma, smelled of cardamom, chocolate, and vanilla. Isobel inhaled deeply as she entered. Holidays at home had smelled like this while she was growing up.

"When are you going to learn to bake these?" Greg Stone stood behind her and rubbed her shoulders.

She leaned into his hands gratefully. "Maybe next month—after we all survive my Thanksgiving dinner—she'll start me on something easy. Mine won't be as good as hers, though."

He dropped a feather-light kiss on her hair. "I'll treasure them more."

Isobel smiled, though he couldn't see her, and looked over the thriving shop. Momma had only opened it this past summer, but it was already one of the most popular stops downtown.

Glass counters formed an ell at the front of the store, displaying piles of baked goodies in neat rows that mimicked the terra-cotta tile floor. At the back of the shop, the kitchen area was open to view, with a large wooden worktable centrally located between shelves, cupboards, and ovens.

Her momma handed a white paper bag across the counter to a customer. "I'm baking more on Tuesday, so stop back by. Better come earlier in the day, though, or I might sell out again."

"I'll do that," he said. "And when will you have the pumpkin cookies?"

"Sometime in the next week, depending on when I can find a good pumpkin. If I bake them Monday or Tuesday, I could set aside a dozen for you."

"I can see whether there are any decent pumpkins at Bigby Farms, Momma," Isobel volunteered.

Bigby Farms had the largest corn maze in the area, as well as hay rides, a pumpkin patch, a petting zoo, and an apple orchard. They would have plenty of pumpkins, and they were Isobel and Greg's next destination.

The customer said, "I heard the Scotts have pumpkins for sale this year."

The Scotts were Drew and Mary Beth Scott, owners of the Scott Christmas Tree Farm. Isobel hadn't heard that they'd put in pumpkins this year, but she remembered Drew telling her the previous winter that they wanted to diversify some more.

"That's an idea. I'll call Mary Beth later," Momma said. "I'll see you on Tuesday, then?"

"I'll be here." The customer smiled at her, nodded stiffly at Isobel and Greg, and left the store.

"You actually mentioned the Bigbys to him?" Momma scolded. "You know he's been fighting their agricultural zoning for years!"

"Oh, was that Mr. Hunt?" Isobel glanced out the glass door, but the customer had already vanished. "I haven't seen him in ages. He's older."

"Aren't we all?" her momma asked. "Still, you didn't have to bring up the Bigbys."

"I wouldn't have if I'd recognized him," Isobel said. "It's just that we're on our way there, so I was thinking about it. The annual pumpkin hunt for the elementary school kids is Monday, and we volunteered to help make sure everything is all set up."

Momma frowned at them over the counter. "Why are you volunteering at the corn maze? You know we have less than two weeks before the big dinner."

Isobel could have pointed out that Momma was spending the entire day at the bakery, so it didn't matter *what* Isobel did with her time. She could have. She didn't.

Instead, she fell back on "I promised Kimberley." Momma would never object to a promise made to a friend—and Kimberley Ansel was Isobel's best friend and former landlady. Kimberley was also the de facto social organizer for the town of River Corners; if there was a special event going on, she had a hand in putting it together and making sure it ran smoothly. Sometimes, that meant recruiting help, such as Isobel and Greg.

"Aren't they going to be busy with customers today?"

She shrugged. "That means we get the chance to see how they normally work, which should make it easier."

"Okay…but no more dead bodies."

"I'm sure we've seen the last of those."

Greg chuckled. "You know the expression that comes to mind, don't you?"

"Yeah, yeah, 'famous last words.' I just want to go on the record as saying if any do show up, it's not my fault."

"Like Michael would believe that." Isobel's cousin Michael was the chief of police in River Corners, and he hadn't been at all happy with her previous involvement in murder investigations.

"Then he should try finding the bodies himself," Isobel said.

She hadn't even found the first body herself, last year on the Scott's Christmas tree farm. She'd just poked around because Michael had arrested her best friend, the aforementioned Kimberley.

"Why should he want you putting yourself in danger?" Momma asked. "That last murderer…"

She didn't have to finish her thought. They all remembered Isobel's kidnapping, and Isobel most certainly did not want to repeat it. Ever. If she did run into a mystery, though, she was pretty certain she wouldn't be able to just walk away. Greg had told her once she couldn't have a cat because she was too similar in temperament to one.

"Enough morbid subjects," her momma declared. "Now, if you two lovebirds are heading out to help Kimberley and the Bigbys get their farm ready, just what did you stop by here for?"

"Breakfast?" Isobel said hopefully.

Momma glowered. "I would hope you'd have something more to eat than my baking. No dessert unless you've had your vegetables."

"Do you have zucchini bread?"

Greg smothered a chuckle and cut into the conversation. "Actually, I told Isobel we should see what time you want her over at your house tonight so we leave the farm in plenty of time."

"Good to see that one of you is sensible!" Momma beamed at Greg.

Isobel could feel the smugness radiating from him. She'd argued for heading to the farm without stopping. After all, Momma would start the lessons whatever time Isobel showed up, early or late, as long as she was home. However, he had insisted. Of course he'd been right.

"So?" Isobel looked at her momma. "What time should I be there?"

"I close at five on Saturdays. You know that."

"I'll be there sometime between five-thirty and six. Am I still cooking the whole dinner?"

A raised eyebrow greeted her question. "You haven't forgotten the menu, have you?"

"Of course not, Momma."

Truthfully, tonight's dinner was well within Isobel's grasp, even if she was famous—or rather, infamous—for her lack of cooking skills: baked ham (already cooked, so she only had to reheat it and glaze it), baked potatoes, and green bean casserole. The only tricky part was managing to cook everything in the two ovens so they finished at the same time. She could do that. It couldn't be any harder than herding freelancers to make sure books went to press and shipped on time, something she managed all the time while working for the River Corners College Press.

It would be the first time Greg had eaten a full meal she'd cooked, however, so she was still nervous.

"So go already," Momma said. "And maybe you can have some cookies for dessert tonight."

Kimberley was in full-on general mode at the Bigby Farm. Folding banquet tables separated the gravel parking lot from the small picnic area and the fields beyond. Labeled bags and boxes in tidy rows covered the tables. Kimberley waved to Isobel and Greg as they crossed the parking lot to where she stood with a clipboard in her hand.

"You're right on time!" She waved toward a small table at the end. "Cider and muffins over there if you need something to eat. The milk crates stacked at the end hold thermoses of coffee—mostly for the spotters, who won't be free to move around. You'll have to run the thermoses out to the spotting stations."

"I'll grab some cider in a minute," Isobel said. "I don't suppose you have hot water to cut it with?"

Kimberley made a face. "I forgot you don't like real cider. Sorry, you're just going to have to drink it as is."

Isobel sighed. "If I must. So what are we doing?" She surveyed the layout. "It looks like you already have everything set up without our help."

"Don't be ridiculous. Do you know how much there still is to do?" Kimberley paused to wave at a family that had just pulled into the parking lot. "Hey, going to see you on Monday?"

The son responded with an enthusiastic "yes," and Kimberley watched them head toward the tractor for the hay ride with a smile on her face. "That's why I do this every year. The kids love it."

"And every year, you have to do more to top the previous year."

Kimberley shrugged. "I don't *have* to, I suppose, but I can't help competing with someone, even if it is only myself. And since the Bigbys are willing to pay for it all…"

Isobel laughed, and Greg said, "Is that why you need us here two days beforehand to set up?"

"Exactly." Kimberley beamed. "Actually, the first order of business is to have fun. Take a map of the maze and work your way through, making sure you visit every single dead end, wrong turn, and spotter station."

"Okay, but why?" Isobel asked.

"Today, it's just for practice and to give you a feeling of the maze. You can take thermoses of coffee out to the spotters while you're at it. On Monday, I'm going to need you to act as a guide, and if the spotters radio in because they've spotted lost kids, you're going to need to go get them out."

"Monday?" Greg looked back and forth between the two women. "I have classes."

Kimberley looked at Isobel. "You didn't tell him to take the day off?"

"It's not that easy for him." She rolled her eyes. "To be fair, Gerri wasn't wild about me taking the time off, either, but at least I don't have students expecting me to show up."

Saying that Gerri Hess, Isobel's boss at River Corners College Press, wasn't wild about it was a bit of an exaggeration. She had looked put upon and asked whether Isobel intended to stay late the rest of the week to make up for it, which was pretty much how she always acted, no matter how busy they were.

"Fine, I'll make do with just you on Monday." Kimberley pointed at Greg. "But you're going to work extra hard on hiding the pumpkins this afternoon to make up for it."

"That's the part I don't get. How do you hide pumpkins? I thought they were all in a wide-open field."

"The real ones are, of course," Kimberley said. "We hide—well, pictures, plastic ones, wood ones, all sorts of different pumpkins. And they can be pretty much anywhere—in the maze, in the gift shop, in the shed where the preschoolers play with the corn."

"We hide them two days before the kids have to find them? What's to stop the kids from looking over the weekend?"

"Nothing," Kimberley and Isobel chorused, grinning at each other.

He looked from one to the other and shook his head. "All right, what aren't you telling me?"

"Monday morning, I replace a random pumpkin with a motion-activated digital camera. Kids who are honestly looking get their picture taken with a look of curiosity. Kids who think they know what to expect tend to look more smug."

Isobel chimed in, "We e-mail a collage to the teachers, of course."

Greg looked thoughtful. "Hmm. I don't think it would do much to discourage a certain curious person I know…"

Isobel gave a put-upon sigh. "Very funny. Come on, let's go check out the maze."

He winked at her and grabbed her hand. "Okay. Should we take coffee out to the spotters?"

Kimberley glanced at her watch. "They haven't been out there that long, but you may as well. I imagine you two are going to take advantage of the wrong turns in the maze."

The Miniature Golf Course Murders

Isobel snorted but didn't bother denying it. Kimberley wouldn't believe her, even if Isobel told her that she and Greg didn't have to sneak around like a pair of teenagers looking for someplace to make out. Of course, Kimberley and Isobel's shared teen years might have something to do with that attitude, even if it had been Kimberley and John sneaking around more than Isobel and Dante.

Several plastic grocery bags were tucked into the milk crates between the thermoses. Greg took two, doubled them up, and placed three thermoses inside. "Is that enough?"

Isobel put one more in the bags, grabbed a map, and said, "Let's go."

According to the map, this year's maze was a stack of half a dozen pumpkins. The entrance was on the other side of the track that the hay ride tractors used. Before crossing, Isobel paused and shaded her eyes, marking the spotter stations mentally. At two of the stations, she saw only silhouettes of the spotters. At a third, a flannel-clad arm waved at her, and she waved back. The fourth station was too far away to make out any details.

Greg paused at the entrance, looking up at the top of the dried corn stalks. "Can those spotters actually see over this?"

"Every year, they manage to find missing children, send in finders to lead out people who are stuck in a loop, and keep an eye out for pranksters."

"And spot people sneaking kisses in secluded corners?" He waggled his eyebrows at her.

"We could find out."

Laughing, they wandered into the maze together.

Having the map made it easier to not get lost, although when they followed one particular route on the maze, they found a split that wasn't on the map. Frowning, Isobel dug a red pen out of her messenger bag and marked the discrepancy. Following the unmarked line, they looped out almost to the edge of the maze—they could see the gravel track just feet away, and the trees on the other side of the track—and then back up to the next higher pumpkin in the stack.

"It spoils the pattern." Isobel frowned.

"Not our problem. Let's keep going."

Soon, they reached the first spotter station. Greg removed a thermos from the bag, set the bag on the ground, and started up the ladder.

A head poked over the edge. "Can I help you?"

"Hey, Marshall!" Isobel waved from the ground. "We're just dropping off some coffee."

"Unless you spiked it with something, I'm not interested."

Wordlessly, Greg reversed his progress on the ladder.

Marshall added, "Noah can probably use mine." He waved off toward his left. "He hasn't been nearly as active as he usually is. Probably because he got in so late last night—or this morning, if you know what I mean."

Isobel was reasonably certain she knew exactly what he meant, but she didn't bother saying so. She didn't care about the personal activities of any of the Bixby boys. She picked up the bag with the thermoses and held it out to Greg so he could put the other one in when he got back down.

Twining their arms together, they set off through the maze once more. They didn't run into anything else that was unexpected, and about fifteen minutes later, they reached the second spotter station. This time, Isobel climbed up.

As her head crested the floor level and she could see into the box area, she gasped. Noah lay on the floor of the station. She sped up. Maybe he was just asleep. Marshall *had* said Noah had been out late the night before. In her heart, she didn't believe it. She was going to have to call her cousin and tell him she'd found another dead body.

Watch for The Corn Maze Murders, *coming in 2014!*

In case you missed the first River Corners Mystery, here's a sample of

THE CHRISTMAS TREE FARM MURDERS

CHAPTER ONE

Tuesday, December 1

Isobel counted out forty-five dollars into Drew Scott's hand. She shivered and drew a little closer to the kerosene heater placed off to the right in the tiny shack. The smell from the heater made her wrinkle her nose.

Drew grinned and waggled his bushy gray eyebrows. "Weather's bitter this year, isn't it? Can't wait to see what January and February bring."

She glowered at the older man. "Do you have to sound like you enjoy it so much?"

He chuckled as he tucked the money into the cash drawer. "Ah, you know I make money selling firewood, too. Pretty as these Christmas trees are, there aren't enough people in the area to make selling them support me and Mary Beth."

"I know. Still, I hate walking home after dark on icy sidewalks."

"That wouldn't be a problem if—" Drew cut himself off as a scream pierced the air. He shoved the cash drawer hard, then pushed past Isobel. The smell of fresh-cut pine cut through the over-heated kerosene in the shack when he opened the door.

Over his shoulder, she saw a couple of the college students he hired as seasonal help in front of the shack talking to Drew's granddaughter, Annie. They were staring off beyond the nearby trees.

"What's going on?" Drew demanded.

The students both shook their heads, but one spoke up. "That sounded like Mrs. Ansel. She was going out to check on the trees she chose for the Christmas pageant—took off on my snowmobile. She'd better bring it back, too, because I have no other way to get home."

Annie nodded emphatically. "That's definitely her voice. I've heard it often enough at rehearsals, though never quite like that."

Isobel blinked. "That sounds rather impulsive for Kimberley." Her friend was meticulous, careful, neat—not impulsive.

The student looked at his feet, and Isobel realized not all the color in his cheeks was from the cold. What did he have to be embarrassed about? "I told her I heard a chainsaw up that way early this morning, and she's afraid her trees may have been poached."

Drew took the rubber-treaded steps two at a time. "No one poaches trees on my farm. I should go see what's going on." He grabbed a set of keys off the rack hanging by the office door. He looked back at Isobel. "One of the lugs over by the fire can get your tree fastened to your car."

She jumped down to stand next to him, stumbling against one of his chainsaw-carved animals that flanked the entry stairs. "No way. Kimberley's my best friend, not just my landlady. If she needs help, well …that's what I'm here for."

He moved over to the nearby tractor and climbed to the driver's seat. "Get on."

The treads churned through the snow. Drew didn't bother sticking to the carefully tended roads. The cold cut into Isobel's throat like a knife, and she wished she'd wrapped up with her scarf before they started.

"How do you know where to go?" She leaned forward and spoke loudly, hoping he'd hear her over the motor.

He yelled back, "I helped Kimberley mark her trees off with ribbon. If we followed the roads, it would take us an extra five minutes to get there."

Isobel opened her mouth, but just then they arced over a mound of snow and landed with jarring force. Her jaw snapped closed, and she was grateful that she hadn't bitten her tongue. She held on and watched over Drew's shoulder for any sign of Kimberley.

They bounced over another obstacle and rounded a bend, sending snow up in waves beside them. Isobel registered the presence of someone in front of them a moment after Drew killed the ignition. They stopped by Kimberley. Isobel looked at her friend with concern. Kimberley was a quiet, efficient, woman who always looked as neat and tidy as her well-kept home did. Right now, her hair looked as though it hadn't seen a brush in weeks. Kimberley's face was flushed and wet, and she struggled to catch her breath.

Isobel hopped off the snowmobile and put her arms around her friend, ignoring the whiff of vomit. "Are you okay? What happened?"

Kimberley shook her head. "Not me. " She pointed toward her trail under the trees. "Back there. It's…it's…why would anyone do that to Laurie?" Her shoulders heaved, and tears flowed down her face.

"What's happened to her?" Isobel asked, drawing back to look at her friend.

"She's dead."

Isobel met Drew's gaze. "Maybe we should see for ourselves. Kimberley, will you be okay here for a couple of minutes?"

Kimberley shook her head. "You don't really want to see this."

Isobel bit her lips. It just seemed so unreal, finding a body here on the Scotts' farm. The call of a cardinal in the trees punctuated the normalcy of the day. As for not wanting to see, how bad could it be?

She eased Kimberley down onto the seat of the snowmobile. "We'll be back soon. Rest here."

Kimberley clutched at Isobel's sleeve. "Please. Just get me to my car. I want to go home."

Isobel gently disengaged Kimberley's fingers from the blue down jacket. "We'll get you back to the parking lot in a little bit, but I can't take Drew's tractor. Just wait here." She stood up. Would Kimberley try to drive herself? She didn't look in any shape to be operating a vehicle. Isobel pocketed the keys to the snowmobile as casually as she could.

Drew had started off through the drifts without her, evidently thinking she would be staying with her friend. As she trudged after him, she gave a half smile. Kimberley had broken through the crust of the snow already, and Drew was clearing a wider path as he followed her trail. Isobel herself wasn't doing much work at all.

The trees to either side had gems of ice on the tips of their needles. The branches were weighted down with inches of snow, except for those places where snow dropped as they passed, making soft plopping sounds and leaving indentations in the snow below. She rubbed her cheeks to remove some of the immobility that had been frozen into them on the wild ride.

Her attention was brought abruptly back to the matter at hand when she bumped into Drew.

"Don't look." He put his right arm out to block her passage. "Kimberley was right enough; the girl is dead."

Given the smells of blood and gas, as well as other, less-identifiable scents, Isobel imagined he was right. However, she was curious, so Isobel ignored his words and ducked under his outstretched arm. She wished she hadn't. Here there was no crystalline beauty of snow. Bits of clothes lay matted with blood, liver, and the contents of the woman's intestines; something had ripped her nearly in two. Isobel tried to focus on the face, to place where she'd seen the woman before. Kimberley had called her by name, but right now, "Laurie" was just a label.

The smell of the body intensified, and Isobel felt the warmth behind her ears that heralded an upsurge of her own stomach's contents. She clamped her lips closed as tightly as she could and turned away from the body. She struggled through the pristine snow, fighting the racking of her body as it tried to rid itself of what she had just seen. Finally, she could hold the tide back no longer.

After she used a little snow to clean her mouth, Isobel walked back to where Drew still stood. He was watching her, and she waved feebly. "I wasn't expecting that." She reached him, careful to focus on his face. "What happened to her?"

"I don't know, but we need to get her some help."

"Help?" Isobel laughed but caught herself before she became hysterical. "I think she's rather beyond help, don't you?" She hesitated. "She is, right? I mean, I don't want to go touch her to check."

He shook his head. "I don't think that's necessary. I'd say Kimberley's right on the money." He nodded off to his left without actually looking that way. "She seems to have had the same reaction that you did, but a lot sooner."

"I had some warning." Isobel looked across the small cleared area. The spot of color on the edge of her vision tugged at her attention, but she refused to look. Instead, she pointed off to one side. "There are tracks leading in and out; maybe it won't be too hard for the police to find out who did this."

Drew followed her gesture and shook his head. "That leads back to the cleared trails and tractor roads. The tracks will get lost there." He paused. "The police?" he asked as though it hadn't already occurred to him.

She raised her eyebrows and stared at him for a moment. When he said nothing further, she said, "Yes, the police. She clearly didn't do this to herself. If you have a cell phone, I'd be willing to make the call for you." She smiled wryly. "I left my cell in my car."

"Phones don't work here. It's a dead zone." He winced as he realized what he had said. He grasped her elbow gently and turned her back the way they had come. "Let's go. We can easily get three on the tractor. With your help, I can even put the snowmobile on the back."

She pulled away from him. She took the keys from her pocket and dropped them into his hand. "You'll go faster with two, and I can keep an eye out so no one else approaches. The snowmobile probably should stay here, at any rate, so the police can say that it's not evidence in the case." She tilted her head to one side. "Would you rather I make the call? It is your farm, but Michael is probably going to start off by asking ridiculous questions like whether you're sure it's murder. I'm used to his skepticism by now."

"No." He patted her on her shoulder. "I appreciate what you're trying to do, but I can remember when your cousin spent his winters here earning a few extra bucks for presents. He's not that big and scary."

Isobel laughed.

"That's better," he said, dropping his hand from her shoulder. "I'll be back as soon as I can. If you see anything even remotely out of place, run and scream."

She nodded. She had no intention of doing otherwise.

Drew and Kimberley disappeared behind the nearest line of trees, and Isobel gnawed at her lips as she watched them go. Good thing she hadn't bothered with lipstick this morning. It would be all over her teeth by now. Was she really safe out here by herself with the corpse? Nothing had happened to Kimberley, she reminded herself. She'd be safe. Of course she would.

Isobel heard the rumble of the tractor returning long before she saw it. It sounded different than it had when it left, and she soon saw why—it was flanked by a pair of snowmobiles. Her cousin Michael's blue fur-trimmed cap was easy to pick out. She held up one hand in greeting.

Michael braked right in front of her, covering her with a load of snow. He glared at her without getting off the machine. "What have you gotten yourself into this time?"

She placed her hands on her hips. Lips compressed, she returned his glare. "I haven't gotten myself into anything. I'm just here to make sure no one disturbed the scene."

"A likely story." He dismounted and stood towering over her. "And the reason you're out here in the first place? Or did it not occur to you that the killer might come back?"

She hadn't thought about that, but it was too late to worry now. She tilted her head up to face him. He knew she hated having to do this; the crick could take days to work out of her neck. "I figured if he didn't come back for Kimberley, he wasn't going to come after me. And somebody had to stay with the body. My momma taught me to help neighbors in need. Maybe I should tell Aunt Rosa she didn't do as good a job with you."

A chuckle from the officer behind Michael was quickly silenced. Her cousin's eyes didn't so much as twitch away from hers at the sound. He poked her nose softly with his finger—more softly than she expected. "And if you turn into the neighbor in need, both our mothers will make my life miserable. So keep out of trouble so I can stay in one piece, huh?"

She took a step back so she didn't have to crane her neck so much to meet his gaze. "If I wanted you to get hurt, I'd invite you over for dinner."

He smiled at that. "I know better than to accept." He rolled his shoulders as he turned away from her. She couldn't blame him for being stressed; River Corners hadn't had a murder since he'd been police chief—probably since he'd been on the force. Well, aside from old Mr. Winters hitting that young salesman with his shotgun because the salesman had smiled at his wife

Isobel sat on the snowmobile that her cousin had been using, facing away from the body. She had no desire to watch the officers investigate the crime scene. Seeing it once had been more than enough. She couldn't get the image of the woman out of her head—body ripped open, but her arms flung out to either side, for all the world as though she had been in the middle of making a snow angel.

Isobel closed her eyes and tried to concentrate on the feel of the breeze pushing her bangs off her face, the scent of pine needles—but, no, that aroma was masked here, and she didn't want to smell the body again.

She listened to the conversation behind her. "When's the coroner going to get here? She was notified before we left." Michael, irritated.

The Miniature Golf Course Murders

"You know Madge. She'll get here when she gets here," another man responded.

Isobel forced herself to stare at the row of trees before her. Was that a spot of red, some songbird, there? If she didn't keep concentrating on the details, she was afraid she'd fall into hysterics.

A warm hand came down onto her shoulder, and Drew said, "If you want, I can run you back to the parking lot. You've been out here long enough."

"I'm going to need a statement before you go home," Michael said.

Isobel leaned to one side to peer past Drew's bulky frame. "Can't you come by and get it later? I promise not to poison you."

He shook his head without smiling. "First twenty-four hours are the most important. The sooner I have all the information, the better."

"What about Kimberley? She found the body. Shouldn't you be getting a statement from her?" She kept her gaze focused on him, trying to ignore the flashes as the other officer moved around the clearing shooting pictures.

"I've already gotten part of her story, and she's waiting back at the pay shack so we can get more details after examining the crime scene." He brushed his hand through his hair. "Drew here can take you back to the shack, but you can't go home yet. And I don't want the two of you talking about what you've seen, or what you think you've seen out here."

"Drew and I, or Kimberley and I?"

He dropped his hand to his side. "I meant you and Kimberley, but I really don't want you talking about this with anyone except me and my officers." The rumble of another tractor cut into his words. It pulled up on the side of the clearing nearer to the road. Isobel saw Michael's hands clench as he headed over to talk to the driver, one of the college students she had seen before. The coroner shoved a faded blue quilt off her lap and shook the snow off of it, then dropped it into a box on the side before she hopped off the trailer and carefully walked around all the paths in the snow to reach the body.

Tall with stringy blond hair, Madge looked and acted casual, hiding the fact that she was quite good at her job. She waved to Isobel then focused her attention on the body. "Yup. She's dead, all right."

Isobel couldn't help it. She giggled. It was just a small giggle at first, but she couldn't stop. She held her stomach and shook with laughter. "Are you okay?" Drew asked her. She shook her head and waved her hand at him but couldn't stop.

A lump of cold snow slid down her neck and into the back of her sweater. She sat upright abruptly, the laughter gone. She looked over her shoulder to see the coroner nod.

"I thought that might help."

"I'm sorry. I don't know what got into me."

The coroner shrugged. "Shock, I'd say. You've been sitting out here in the cold watching a dead body. I don't know what our vaunted police chief was thinking, but I imagine he's going to get an earful from your mother."

"Vaunted? Who's been doing any vaunting? I've just been trying to do my job. I'm already calling in every off-duty person and even a few retirees. I don't have the manpower to do this any better." Michael stomped back through the snow toward her. A trace of concern crossed his face. "You don't look so good. Drew can take you back to the shack now. Remember, don't talk about this with anyone."

Isobel nodded numbly. She wanted to make a crack about whether she was allowed to leave town, but the words wouldn't come.

The coroner added, "And be sure to have something hot to drink while you're waiting."

Back at the parking lot, Isobel saw that the students had done a good job of fastening her tree to the roof of her car. Maybe too good. She'd have to remember to ask them how she was supposed to get it back off.

She stepped down from the tractor and rubbed her upper arms slowly. She probably should have used one of those quilts, the way Madge had on her tractor ride.

Drew gave her a nudge in the small of her back, and she let him guide her up the stairs to the shack.

"It's about time!" Kimberley exclaimed as they entered the shack. "Oh. It's you. I assumed it was your overbearing cousin who told me to stay put until he comes back." She pushed herself back up against the cash register to make space in the tiny room. "As though I have nothing better to do while he goes off to look at...at...Isobel, this is so awful!" She threw her arms around her friend. "Who could have done such a thing?"

Isobel hugged Kimberley, patting her on the back as she would a small child to calm it. Or so she supposed. She'd never had any to care for herself, and unlike most girls, she had never gone in for babysitting as a teen. "We can't talk about that right now. We have to wait and talk to the police first."

Kimberley leaned back without letting go of her. "I suppose your cousin said that as well, didn't he? What gives him the right to be so high-handed? You'd think he'd been quarterback of the football team in high school or something."

Isobel gave a small smile, careful not to laugh again. "Instead of the star tackle?" She inched closer to the heater. She could feel the blood coming back into her cheeks, but the tip of her nose still felt frozen, and her fingers were stiff. How could she ever spend time reading slush—unsolicited manuscripts—for the press tonight when she felt like her fingers would never move again? Well, there was always more slush. Maybe a hot bath was the better plan.

"Eh." Kimberley dismissed Michael with a deprecating sound. "I didn't notice anyone on the team except for John. You know that."

Drew cleared his throat. "You need something to drink. Coffee okay?"

At the mention of coffee, Isobel's stomach felt queasy again. "I don't think I need the caffeine right now. Maybe some of the cider you keep for the kids?" He nodded and stepped outside the shack.

As soon as he left, Kimberley released Isobel. "He's gone. So tell me—who do you think killed her? Who do they think killed her?"

"I told you before, I can't talk about this now. After Michael releases us and we go home, I'll be happy to talk as much as you want. But not right now."

"Do you have to follow lock-step in every little thing that your family wants you to do?"

"You didn't seem to think that was such a bad thing when Momma and Aunt Rosa ganged up on me to get me to stay here in town when I wanted to head off upstate to get a job with a larger press."

The door opened again before Kimberley could make a come-back. Drew carried a Styrofoam cup in each of his hands. "I thought you might want something, too, Kimberley. I can't believe you haven't been given anything yet."

Isobel accepted the cider from Drew with a smile. Heat seeped through the cup into her fingers. "This smells wonderful." She sighed happily. "And I think my hands are actually starting to thaw again."

Kimberley arched an eyebrow at her. "I've told you before you need something more substantial than those driving gloves."

"I know. I just like to save my winter wool until at least the first official day of winter." Isobel took a sip. The cider was from a package mix with very little cinnamon dissolved in scalding water. She breathed through her mouth for a moment to let her tongue cool. Just the way she liked it, though she'd have taken just about anything to clean her mouth right now.

She glanced at Drew. "Any sign of Michael and his officers coming back?"

He shook his head. "I'll go keep an eye out. If anyone else comes to pick up their Christmas tree, I'll steer them in a different direction."

A gust of wind blew the door out of his hand, slamming it against the wall. Drew swore, then looked at the pair of women. "Sorry." He walked down the steps and carefully closed the door behind him.

As soon as he was gone, Kimberley set down the cup he had handed her. "Honestly, I don't understand how you can drink that stuff. He dilutes it to make it go farther, you know."

Isobel shrugged and took a step away from the heater.

"I hope your cousin gets back soon," Kimberley said. "I need to get back to work."

Neither of them said anything more.

When Michael finally opened the door, Isobel felt the atmosphere inside the shack was almost as frosty as that outside. "I was beginning to think you'd forgotten us," she said, moving forward.

Kimberley pushed past her. "It's about time. Can I give you my statement now so I can go back to someplace more civilized, like my shop which has been closed for several hours with a 'will return in 30 minutes' sign hanging on the front door?"

"Actually, ladies, you're going to have to wait a few more minutes. I don't do shorthand, so we're going to wait for an officer who does. He was off-shift and hasn't gotten here yet. He'll take down the statements and transcribe them later. You'll be called in to the station to read and sign your statements when he's done. While we're waiting," he continued, "can either of you give me an unofficial identification of the victim so we can see about notifying the next-of-kin?"

"Her name—she's Laurie Anderson. She is—was—the secretary in the history department." Kimberley gulped audibly. "Her sister's on campus somewhere. John would know."

Isobel wrapped an arm around her friend. The history department? That must be why the woman had seemed vaguely familiar. Isobel would have seen her on campus or at one of John and Kimberley's parties.

Kimberley pulled away. She looked as though she wanted to stalk off in a huff, but there was nowhere to go with barely room for three people to stand in the shack. "I just want this to be over so I can go back to work. I don't see why I can't write down what I saw and go. It's not like there's any question that she was dead, with her body all—"

"Sorry. Those are the regulations." Michael cut her off. "You two really shouldn't have been left alone with each other, either, but I don't have the manpower to deal with this."

Kimberley sniffed. "Perhaps next time you'll let me handle the bond campaign for better funding."

Trust Kimberley to try to turn this into more work for herself, not that the bond was a bad idea. It might even keep Kimberley's mind off what she'd seen, but Michael needed to deal with the here-and-now, not some future political issue.

Isobel took pity on her cousin. "If I promise not to talk to anyone, can I go outside and stretch my legs? Maybe get another cup of cider?" She gestured with the cup that she still held.

He hunched to one side to give her room to pass. "I suppose I can be lenient since you haven't tried to climb out the window."

"It's the coat. It would never fit."

"While you're out there," he said, "talk to the officers by the tape. They need footprints to compare to the crime scene."

Isobel glanced down at her feet, then at Kimberley's. "I hope you're not hoping brand will be a clue. Half the town wears these."

"Just do it, Isobel. Please."

After giving the officers the requested footprints, Isobel got herself another cup of the cider and drank it down quickly—too quickly, as it scalded her throat, which already felt raw. She refilled her cup and sipped at it more reflectively, watching the tendrils of steam curling in the air. One of Drew and Mary Beth's cats wrapped itself around her legs, and she squatted to pet it. Michael had stayed by the door to the shack, and the college students were huddled around the fire, nudging each other but not saying anything she could hear.

It was good to get out of the shack, but the tension wasn't going away. She didn't think it would anytime soon, not even at home. She glanced at the shack nervously. She and Kimberley were getting on each other's nerves. Maybe it was time for her to think about moving out on her own. The in-law cottage was nice, but she was still conscious of effectively being under someone else's roof. She blew on her cup of cider and watched the ripples bouncing across its surface. When this mess got straightened out, she'd have to start looking.

"Is my grandpa in trouble?" Annie had come up to stand next to her.

Isobel shook her head. "He didn't do anything wrong."

He hadn't, had he? Drew didn't mix with the people of the college, so Isobel couldn't imagine where he would have met the dead woman before she showed up here. Far likelier that Laurie had come to the farm with her murderer, someone who took advantage of the circumstances to leave the body in an out-of-the-way place.

"I wish my mom were here." Annie's mom, a journalist and the Scotts' pride and joy, was a journalist, embedded with the troops in the Middle East. The last thing Annie needed to worry about was losing more of the adults in her life.

Isobel tried to reassure the fifteen-year-old. "Your grandpa can take care of himself. And if he can't, you and your grandmother can pick up the slack. You'll be fine."

Annie thrust out her lips in a practiced pout. "I'd be better if someone told me what's going on, but the police aren't saying anything—just scaring off the customers."

Isobel glanced at the parking lot, startled, and realized it was true. A cruiser with its lights flashing parked across the entrance, blocking any cars that might have approached. Another sat next to the exit, an officer with a clipboard standing beside it, taking information—names, she guessed—from those leaving.

"I'm sure they'll tell everyone what's happening soon," Isobel said.

"Yeah, right." Annie thrust her hands into her pockets. "I'd better go see if Grandma needs my help for anything."

Isobel watched the girl slouch away, glad that Annie, at least, had been spared the sight of the body in the snow. Isobel rehearsed over and over in her mind what to say.

Once the other officer arrived, things went rather quickly. Isobel deferred to Kimberley, as her friend had been the one to find the body. Isobel gave her statement in as few short, well-crafted sentences as she could. Michael prompted her a few times with questions, but she didn't really have anything to add. The body was dead when they got there, she hadn't touched it, she hadn't seen anyone else touch it.

"But you did get sick all over."

She gave a long-suffering sigh. "Yes, I did. At least I kept it away from the body."

"Considerate of you."

At last, Michael nodded. "You can go now. I'll let you know when the statement is ready to sign."

"I'll try to make sure Momma doesn't flay you in the meantime. Yours, I can't guarantee. You know they're going to blame you."

He snorted. "As if you can guarantee Aunt Maria Elena."

If you enjoyed this sample, pick up The Christmas Tree Farm Murders *at your favorite e-book store. (Also available in paperback!)*

Printed in Great Britain
by Amazon